FORGET-ME-NOTS FOR FELICITY

For Mom

In loving memory

Contents

Chapter One

May 11, 1857

Upper Pangford, England

Felicity Wixom shivered as she set her canvas on an easel in the garden. Her chosen spot this morning was a patch of lawn bordered by flower beds. A hedgerow on one side divided this part of the garden from the more extensive grounds. Spring in Upper Pangford was cool and often rainy, but today the sky was mostly clear. She was grateful for the coat she wore over her dress and apron. Her skirt soaked up dew from the grass, but the crinoline kept the fabric away from her legs.

While the servants were awake and busy, the members of her family were still sleeping. She preferred to paint when no one was around because she was all too aware of what the family thought of her endeavors. Mother informed her there were more suitable pastimes for a lady: delivering food baskets to the less fortunate, stitching embroidery, and playing music. Felicity, however, refused to spend hours toiling over the pianoforte when she had neither the proclivity nor the skill.

A servant set up a small table next to the easel and placed her box of paints on it. "Will there be anything else, Miss Wixom?"

"No, thank you. When I am finished, I'll let you know," she said.

The young man rubbed his cold hands together before bowing and dashing back to the relative warmth of the manor. Felicity took a pencil from her box and quickly sketched some forget-me-nots on the canvas. Her touch was light, her lines sure. She squinted at the small blossoms, concentrating on the shape of the shadows beneath the blue flowers and between the green leaves. Getting the shadows right made all the difference in the world.

When the sketch was done, she squeezed paint from the tin tubes onto her palette: Prussian blue, cobalt blue, white, yellow ochre, emerald green, and umber. She worked quickly to get everything ready before the morning sun was high enough to shine over the garden hedge and touch the edges of the blue forget-me-nots. They were her favorite flowers, and they were at their finest this week. Gray clouds drifted across the sun for a moment, and she glared at them, as if she could make them move out of the way.

Felicity mixed paint and rapidly applied a thin layer of a rusty-brown color on her canvas. Next, she mixed the shades of blue and green she needed for the flower petals and leaves. Yellow and white would mimic the sunlight hitting the edges of the petals. The clouds parted, allowing the sun's rays to kiss the pale blue blossoms, edging them in gold. Felicity set to work and was soon absorbed in the rhythm of her brushstrokes. This was her favorite escape from all the pressures of society. If she had her way, she would turn down every invitation to a ball, a party, or afternoon tea. Life was simpler here with her paints and her plants.

She forgot the cold morning air and was completely oblivious to the songbirds flitting around the garden. A gentle breeze made the flowers sway, much to her consternation. It was challenging enough to get the lighting right without the flowers moving. She bit her lip as she worked, a wrinkle creasing her brow.

It was the eternal challenge of a painter, always chasing the light, trying to adequately express its qualities on canvas, racing to finish before the sun moved too much and everything changed. She didn't often succeed, but that did not stop her trying.

Felicity longed for some formal training, but the one time she'd approached Father about applying to the Female Academy of Art in London, he had refused to consider it. He didn't complain about her spending her pin money on paints and art supplies, but there his support ended. She had not told anyone except her friend, Louisa, about her ambition to have a painting accepted in the new summer exhibition hosted by the Society of

Female Artists. When Louisa had gone to London last month, she had taken one of Felicity's paintings to enter. Now all she could do was wait to hear if her work was accepted.

Soon the forget-me-nots would be in full sun and her attempts to capture the angled light would have to wait until tomorrow. She did not rush, however. She would not sacrifice accuracy to the demands of speed. She hoped this painting would be her best yet.

"Forget-me-nots again?" A male voice startled her, and Felicity jumped, her brush making an errant stroke across the canvas.

She turned to her older brother in frustration. "Edmund! Look what you've done!" Grabbing a rag, she swiped at the paint streak.

"It wasn't me. You are the one with the brush."

"You startled me. You shouldn't go around sneaking up on people."

"I was hardly sneaking," Edmund said. "You enter your own world when you paint and it's not my fault you didn't hear me."

Still, he could have given her some warning. "You have the grace of a lumbering bull. I'm surprised you managed to be so quiet," she said, focusing on her work.

"When are you going to paint something besides flowers?" Edmund asked.

"Like what?"

"Like me." Edmund struck a pose, one hand on an imagined cane, the other tipping his hat.

Felicity glared at him. "You couldn't hold still long enough for me to paint you."

"I can too."

"Prove it. Stand in that pose right now while I finish up this flower."

She focused on her painting. Today, the work was going better than usual. The blue flowers were just the right shade, and the shadows gave the leaves and petals dimension.

"What gets you out of bed so early?" Felicity asked. Edmund usually slept as late as he possibly could.

He scuffed the ground with the toe of his boot. But instead of asking her something, as she anticipated, he said," I thought I would take a walk," and ambled off down the garden path.

"I knew you couldn't hold a pose," she called after him as he wandered off. He waved a hand at her.

Something must be on his mind for, although he was to inherit the entire estate of Ashwick Manor, he rarely came to the garden. She wondered what it was.

Felicity continued painting until gray, foreboding clouds blocked the sun. She hurried to wrap her brushes in a cloth and tucked them inside her painting box. She'd clean them properly after breakfast. Despite the impending rain, she arranged her paint tubes neatly within the box and plucked a few forget-me-nots from the garden to bring inside.

As she lifted her painting from the easel, a raindrop splashed against her cheek. She was careful not to let the painting touch her skirts because she did tend to get paint on everything.

"Let me help." Edmund surprised her as he handed her the paint box. He folded the easel, tucked it under one arm, and picked up the little table. "Let's get out of the rain."

Felicity hurried down the path toward the house, her boots crunching on the gravel. Wind made her skirt billow upward and she tried to hold it in place with the weight of her paint box. A second gust tore at the canvas in her hand.

"Give me the box," Edmund said.

She relinquished it and gripped the canvas with both hands, tilting the painted side toward the ground to protect it from stray raindrops. As rain pelted her in earnest, Felicity darted to the servants' entrance and burst inside the scullery. Edmund bumped into her with his load and the easel clattered to the floor. Felicity flinched, hoping it was not damaged. At least he hadn't dropped her paint box.

He propped the folded table and the easel against the wall and put her paint box on a counter. "We made it," he said, brushing drops of rain from his face.

"Yes, thanks to you." Felicity examined the painting and was relieved it had survived their rushed trip back to the house.

She longed for the day that the glass addition would be completed. She'd be able to paint in the shelter of the conservatory to her heart's content. Father planned to have steam heat in the room to accommodate tropical plants. It would be smaller than the Palm House at Kew Gardens, and insignificant when compared to the Crystal Palace, but it would be the only one in Upper Pangford.

Edmund stopped her before she could take the painting upstairs. "Wait, Fliss. I need a favor. Please."

"You know I don't like it when you call me that," Felicity said.

"We've always called you that," Edmund frowned. "Ever since we were children."

"In case you haven't noticed, I'm not a child anymore."

"*Felicity,*" he said, placing an emphasis on her name. "Will you please do me a favor?"

"I suppose I should grant you one since you did rescue my easel and paints from the storm."

Edmund grinned. "I knew I could count on you. A young lady has caught my eye, and I want you to help me court her. I don't want to make a mess of things this time."

The last time Edmund fancied someone, he had lacked all tact in his approach. He had not only tossed stones at the young lady's bedroom window to get her attention, but had also followed her so close during a garden party that he had stepped on her dress, causing it to tear. The young lady's father intervened, demanding that Edmund leave his daughter alone. After that experience, Edmund had limited his social engagements, but lately, he had been venturing out in society with greater frequency. Now Felicity understood why.

"What would that involve, exactly?" she asked.

"I would like you to accompany me to social engagements and give me advice on how to act and how to talk to her."

"You don't need me for that. Be polite and be yourself," she said, setting the forget-me-nots in water.

"I do need your help. I don't know whether I should call on her, or write her a letter, or ask her to dance." Edmund held her gaze, pleading in his eyes. "I can't ask Silas since he's in India, and I still think of Lucy as a baby sister."

"Lucy is eighteen. She is hardly a baby," Felicity said, not wanting to admit that she still thought of Lucy as a baby sister, too.

"Have you heard from Silas?" Felicity asked. Silas Parker was Edmund's best friend.

"I haven't. But even if he were here and I could talk to him, you are more observant and know best what might work with a young lady," Edmund said.

"What is her name?" Felicity asked.

"I'd rather not say."

"Then I cannot be of help to you, Edmund. Every lady is different. Besides, society and I are not on speaking terms. Perhaps you and I are doomed to being alone." She opened her paint box and carried her brushes to the sink.

"I don't believe that, and neither do you. You haven't met the right person yet," he said.

That was true enough, for although she had fully participated in a few seasons now, she had never met anyone who was easy to talk to. Someone who made her laugh. Someone, she admitted, like Silas Parker. He was the standard by which she judged all other men.

"Please, Fliss," Edmund continued. "I am not the only one competing for her affection."

Felicity paused. "Do you do that to annoy me?"

Silas was the one who first called her Fliss, and he was the only one she allowed to still call her that.

"No. Sorry."

"You said other men were courting her. How do they act?"

"They are very brazen with their behavior toward her," Edmund said. "I cannot compete with them."

"Nor should you. You must be subtle."

"Subtle? How will that get her attention?"

Felicity gave him an exasperated sigh. "It will get her attention because you will be different from all the rest. I think a conservative approach is best if you think she is worth the effort. I recommend you start with a friendly bouquet of flowers that hints of something more."

"I have no idea how to do that," he said.

She finished cleaning her brushes and washed her hands. "We shall go to the flower shop together." She liked the flower shop and visiting it with Edmund would give her an excuse to see what plants she might want for the conservatory once it was finished.

"Now?" Edmund asked.

"Not now. This afternoon, if the rain lets up. I want to eat breakfast, and I'll need to change out of my painting clothes."

"You won't regret it, Felicity. I promise," Edmund said.

Edmund was insufferable at times, but she did love him. Although she did not look forward to a summer of social events that took time away from her painting, she would make the sacrifice for him. She carried the painting up to her bedroom and leaned it against the wall. In the subdued light from her window, the picture showed promise.

She changed into dry clothes and glanced in the mirror, smoothing a tendril of hair. Her gaze fell on the letter she'd left out lying on her vanity. It was from Silas, and it was over a month old. She had written to him regularly, even sent him a Valentine in February, but she had heard very little from him in return. It frustrated her, because while he was Edmund's best friend, he was her friend, too. She wondered how much longer it would be until he returned. His presence made the neighborhood events so much more tolerable. She tucked the letter back in her drawer and headed downstairs for breakfast.

When she entered the breakfast room, Father had already eaten, as evidenced by the newspaper left on the table. Felicity idly turned the pages when an advertisement caught her eye. It was for the Society of Female Artists show beginning June first.

If her painting was accepted into the exhibit, Father would have to take her art seriously. The possibility raced through her like a spring storm, bringing both excitement and trepidation. She tried to remember their last conversation about art. Had he expressly forbidden her to exhibit her art anywhere, or had he only refused to let her apply to school? If her painting got in the exhibit, she would worry about Father's reaction then. Fingers trembling, she folded the paper and set it back on the table.

Chapter Two

May 11, 1857

Delhi, India

It was hot, even this early in the morning. Silas Parker mopped his forehead with a handkerchief and wondered if he would ever be dry again as he made his way from his bunga-low to Mr. Talbot's home. It was as if the air was a cup of warm tea. If he ever advanced to a higher position in the East India Company, he might be able to spend the hottest months in the mountains with the generals and high-ranking civil servants, but for now, as a lowly clerk, he was stuck here.

Mr. Talbot was head of the local office, and normally Silas went to work in the offices near the royal palace. But today, as he sometimes did, Mr. Talbot had asked Silas to review papers at his home before he left Delhi for some meetings. A servant let him in and directed him to the room that Mr. Talbot used as a study. Mr. Talbot was not in the room, and Silas supposed he was taking his usual morning walk around the garden. On some mornings, he even invited Silas to accompany him.

The air stirred, and he glanced up to see the large, rectangular punkah in motion. The punkah-wallah pulled the cord in a steady rhythm, making the fabric flap to stir the air. This morning, it was Rakesh, dressed in the typical style: belted white tunic, white pants, and a turban on his head. Silas nodded at him in gratitude. He had been in the Talbot's home often enough that he was well acquainted with the staff. He still found it unnerving how the servants moved so silently about the house that he often did not hear them entering the room.

Upon his arrival in India, Silas was shocked at the denigrating way some of the British men interacted with the native people they employed, and he was relieved that Mr. Talbot treated everyone with respect, including the lowest members of the staff. Silas made every effort to do the same.

He opened his case and laid out the contracts for Mr. Talbot to review. His job was not very demanding, but Silas preferred it that way. He navigated this position as he did much of his life...with as little effort as possible. A dirt-smudged, crumpled letter slid out from among the papers and to his surprise, it was addressed to him in Miss Felicity Wixom's familiar handwriting. He hadn't noticed it before. It must have been mixed up with the other papers at the office. He fingered the letter, impressed that it had found its way from England all the way to Delhi.

He was always eager for news from home, and Felicity was his most reliable correspondent. Dear Felicity. She was the younger sister of his best friend, Edmund, and although he was four years older, they had shared many childhood adventures.

Shouts from outside tore his attention away from the letter. He tucked it into the pocket of his waistcoat and hurried to the window to see what was happening. The street was clear. Whoever was causing the ruckus was not in sight.

Rakesh had stopped fanning, his attention also on the noises outside. It made Silas uneasy. Were tempers flaring in the heat, or were the rumors of a larger unrest true? As he resumed his seat behind the desk, he glanced at Rakesh. He couldn't read the man's expression, but under Silas's gaze, the punkah-wallah set the fan in motion once again.

"Mr. Parker." Mrs. Talbot, the wife of his employer, entered the room unannounced. Nine-year-old Charlie in his knickers and jacket followed her, holding four-year-old Hannah by the hand. Hannah, with her blond curls in ringlets and wearing a green dress that reached just below her knees, was a miniature version of her mother. "I am looking for Charles. Have you seen him?" Mrs. Talbot asked.

Silas rose. "He asked me to meet him here this morning, but I haven't seen him. Have you checked the garden?"

She frowned and twisted a handkerchief in her hands. "He was not in the garden. I have received word from the office that there is a disturbance near the palace, and I am worried that the mutiny has spread here from Meerut. Are we safe here?"

Silas returned to the window. Indian men on horses in cavalry uniforms were skirmishing with British officers in the street, not far from the Talbot residence. If the mounted sowars were the first wave of an attack, things were going to get worse. He hesitated.

"I'm sure Mr. Talbot will be here any moment. He'll know what to do," Silas said. A flicker of panic started in his chest and his pulse quickened. Not only did Silas not want to deal with a mutiny, but he also did not want to be responsible for anyone else should trouble arise.

Mrs. Talbot peered out the window, where more armed men joined the fray. She gasped as two sowars turned on a British man with their bayonets. Silas put his hand on her arm and steered her away from the sight.

"Should we go to the Main Guard, or should we wait for Charles?" Mrs. Talbot asked.

Indecision filled him. He was unarmed, and the rebels could break into the house at any moment. The Main Guard had fifty soldiers stationed there and was at the north end of the city, near the Kashmir gate. If they left now, they could be under the soldiers' protection within a few minutes. While he would prefer to wait for Mr. Talbot, time was of the essence. He could go for help, but he could not, in good conscience, leave a woman and her children behind.

"Gather what you need for the children. Hats and some food. Whatever you can carry comfortably. We must leave at once."

Hannah gazed up at him through tear-filled eyes, her lower lip trembling. "I want Papa," she said.

Mrs. Talbot knelt beside the girl "We shall wait for him."

Silas shook his head. "You saw how things are outside. I don't believe waiting here is advisable."

Shouts accompanied pounding on the front door of the house. Mrs. Talbot looked at him in alarm.

Silas swallowed hard. "Wait here."

He closed the office door, leaving her and the children in the room. The hall was empty as he rushed to the main entrance of the house. Two of the servants were using a dresser and a table to barricade the door. "Where is Sahib?" they asked him, meaning Mr. Talbot.

"I don't know.," Silas said. If someone from the streets was intent on getting inside the house, he wondered how long the barrier would hold. He needed to do something, and quickly. "I am going to take Mrs. Talbot and the children to the Main Guard."

"Would you like us to get the cart ready?"

"Yes, when you have finished here," Silas said.

Mrs. Talbot entered the hall, Charlie and Hannah trailing after her. "Is there any word from Charles?"

Silas shook his head.

"You must go, Memsahib," one of the servants said as shouts and pounding continued outside the door. "We don't know how long we can protect you and the children here."

Hannah began to cry in earnest. Mrs. Talbot scooped up her daughter. "Shhh, darling. We'll go with Mr. Parker, and he will keep us safe until your father comes for us."

"I can't leave Marietta," Hannah wailed.

Silas raised a quizzical eyebrow.

"Her doll," Mrs. Talbot explained.

"Fetch the doll and whatever else you need. Charlie and I will gather supplies from the kitchen," Silas said.

"If it is so urgent, we can leave now. We'll get the doll when we return."

Silas, not wanting to further alarm the children, gave her a slight shake of his head. Realization dawned on her face.

"We aren't coming back?" Mrs. Talbot's voice was barely above a whisper.

"You should get the doll," Silas said.

He took Charlie by the hand. "Help me get some food, and we'll have a little adventure, shall we? You'll have a grand story to tell your father."

Mrs. Talbot grasped his arm. "How will Charles find us?"

Silas placed his hand over hers, trying to offer reassurance. "Once we are safe, we will figure out how to send word to him."

When Silas entered the kitchen, he recognized Ishaan and Arun, two of the male servants. They were standing in the corner, speaking with two other men in hushed tones. Everyone stopped talking when they saw him, and the two strangers fled the kitchen.

"Who were those men?" Silas asked.

"Friends," Arun said.

Silas wanted to ask the men for more information, but he was keenly aware of Charlie standing beside him.

Ishaan stepped forward. "They bring rumors of sowars heading toward the Main Guard."

"I saw cavalry in the street. Were those sowars from here in Delhi?" Silas asked. If they were locals, maybe they would stand up against the mutineers.

Ishaan shook his head. "From Meerut."

Cavalry from Meerut meant the mutineers were heading for the Main Guard, and it would not be safe for Mrs. Talbot and her children to head there.

"What about the Kashmir Gate?" Silas asked.

Arun shook his head. "I would not try it, Sahib."

If the Kashmir Gate was out of the question, they would need to head further west. The Kabul Gate was not far. Silas wished once again that Mr. Talbot were here to take charge of the situation. Why had he requested Silas meet him at his home today if he wasn't going to be there? The thought gave him pause. Had Mr. Talbot sensed the rising unrest and wanted someone here for his family? If so, Silas had no choice but to take care of them.

"We need food," Silas said. "Will you pack some for Mrs. Talbot and the children?"

Ishaan sprang into action. He grabbed a basket, lined it with a cloth, and filled it with bread, fruit, and jars of chutney. He added some flasks of water and a few sweets before handing the basket to Silas.

"It will not be enough for more than a few days," Ishaan warned.

Silas paused in the kitchen doorway, wondering if he would ever return to this house. The Natives outnumbered the British here, and he doubted the East India Company could hold the location. "Thank you for everything, Ishaan, Arun. Will you be safe here?" he asked. He had no idea how the rebellion would impact the people employed by the British.

Ishaan spoke softly in his heavily accented English. "We will be safe. You must stay away from the main road and the bazaar."

Silas nodded. "Come, Charlie, let's join your mother." He ushered the boy out the back door into the garden where Mrs. Talbot and Hannah were waiting. Mrs. Talbot carried a valise, and Hannah had her doll clutched in her arms.

"We have food," Charlie announced.

Mrs. Talbot forced a smile. "Well done. Now, you must listen to me, and to Mr. Parker on this adventure. Whatever we tell you to do, you must do it with no questions." She met Silas's gaze, her eyes wary.

Silas patted Charlie's shoulder. "Yes. That is the rule of the game. Are you ready?"

"Yes," Charlie said.

Silas led them to the garden gate. The pleasant scent of the flowers was in stark contrast to the seriousness of their situation. The cart and bullock were waiting outside and the animal snorted as they approached. Silas helped the children into the back of the cart, nodding to the older man standing at the animal's head.

"Where are you going, Sahib?" the man asked. Silas struggled to remember his name. Finally, it came to him. Ishaan's father, Mahendra.

"Do you know the opening in the wall between the Kashmir Gate and the Morre Gate?" Silas asked.

Mahendra nodded.

Silas pressed several rupees in his hand. "Please take us there."

"I want to go to the Main Guard," Mrs. Talbot said.

"Trust me, Mrs. Talbot. We need to get to the Flagstaff Tower."

"Outside the city?"

"Yes, and as quickly as possible." Silas lifted the children into the cart and offered Mrs. Talbot his hand. She took it and got into the cart next to Hannah. Silas climbed in and stretched out near Charlie. "Don't make a sound," he said.

Mohendra covered them with piles of laundry. Silas struggled to breathe under the suffocating layer of sheets and towels. He wanted to claw out of the pile and run for the city wall.

Mrs. Talbot seemed to sense his panic. She tented a bit of towel, making an opening near his head. He turned his face toward it, inhaling deeply until he regained his composure. The cart jerked into motion and Charlie reached for his hand.

The cart bumped and jostled them, and the ride was far from comfortable. Beads of sweat rolled down his face and back. Charlie whispered, "How much longer?"

"Not long," Silas said, although he had no idea how long the journey would take, or if they would make it.

Men shouted, and the cart stopped. Mrs. Talbot hugged Hannah close. He heard Mohendra speaking but could not understand what he was saying. The shouting grew louder, and rocks rained down on them with a force that made Silas grateful for the protection of the towels. To his relief, the cart started moving once again.

It was a harrowing journey, and Silas lost all sense of direction as the cart made its way through twisting streets. Finally, they stopped, and Mohendra uncovered them.

"Are we there?" Charlie asked.

Silas shook his head. "Once we leave the city, we must climb to the tower."

"I cannot go further," Mohendra said. The opening was not wide enough to accommodate the cart.

"We shall go on foot. Thank you for getting us this far," Silas said. He peered through the opening and was relieved that no one was in sight.

"Won't Charles wait for us at the Main Guard?" Mrs. Talbot asked, joining him at the wall.

Silas shook his head. "Not if he has any sense, and I believe that he does. No British citizen will be safe there while this uprising continues." He took the valise and the basket of food.

Mohendra had already turned the cart around and was heading back into the city when they passed through the opening in the wall. Silas scanned the surrounding area. Flagstaff Tower was visible in the distance, atop the North Ridge. He could alert the telegraph operators there to send for help. A narrow footpath ran from the wall toward the ridge and Silas hoped it would lead them to a larger road.

Charlie tugged on his arm. "I'm thirsty. When can we stop?"

"See that tower at the top of the ridge? Once we get there, we'll have something to drink. It won't be much longer," he said, hoping he was right. The heat was brutal under the unrelenting sun. His legs shook, and he was thirsty, too, but they had to keep going.

The path did indeed lead to a wider dirt road. Silas saw other people ahead of them, making their way to the tower. He also saw women and children lining the path, yelling as people passed by.

"Steady, Charlie. When we get to those people, we shall have a foot race." He shifted the valise and basket to one hand and scooped up Hannah with his other arm. "And you, Miss Talbot, shall have a ride." He settled Hannah on his hip, and she clung to him and her doll.

As they neared the group, people yelled insults and hurled rocks. Mrs. Talbot gathered her skirts and broke into a run, Charlie close behind her. Silas tried to shield Hannah, but it was impossible as people lined both sides of the path. He ran as fast as he could manage carrying the child and the bags.

A rock caught him on the forehead, but he ignored the sharp pain and continued to run from the crowd. Blood and sweat ran into his eye, but he didn't have a free hand to wipe it away. He held onto Hannah and kept running. Mrs. Talbot and Charlie slowed, and Silas called encouragement to them. They must make it past the villagers.

Charlie ran forward again, and to his relief, Mrs. Talbot followed.

When the last of the crowd finally gave up the chase, Silas set Hannah down and used a handkerchief to staunch the flow from the cut on his forehead.

"Does it hurt?" Hannah asked.

"Yes," Silas said. "But we need to keep going. See, there's your mother."

When they reached Mrs. Talbot, he sank to the ground, his head throbbing.

"Let me look," she said. He took the handkerchief away and was alarmed at the sight of it, and his hand, bright red with his blood. Mrs. Talbot's fingers were gentle as she examined the wound. "Let's bandage it up and we'll take another look at it when we get to the tower," she said.

She folded a clean handkerchief and had him hold it against his forehead while she tore a strip of cloth from her skirt and tied the bandage in place.

Mrs. Talbot picked up the valise and basket. "Charlie, hold onto your sister and stay by me. Come, Mr. Parker, let's get to the tower."

He wished for shade, but encouraged by her bravery, he got to his feet and kept walking. He longed for a wash basin, and a clean bed.

When they reached the tower, Silas was relieved that it was still manned by British personnel. Mrs. Talbot had him sit with the children in a bit of shade. She pulled a flask out of the basket and gave them each a drink of water.

"Your wound has not soaked through the bandage," she said. "I think you will be all right."

"I should return to Delhi and look for Mr. Talbot," Silas said.

"No, Mr. Parker. Please don't leave us," Mrs. Talbot said. "We've nowhere to go, and I cannot manage this without you."

Silas gazed back at Delhi. Smoke rose over the city in gray columns. He was torn between the desire to find Mr. Talbot and his obligation to the Talbot family. If he returned to Delhi, he was unarmed and not likely to be of much use in the conflict. Mr. Talbot would want him to take care of Mrs. Talbot and the children.

"I won't leave you," he said.

Chapter Three

May 11, 1857

Upper Pangford, England

Felicity entered the flower shop with Edmund following close behind. To her relief, the shop was empty this afternoon. A bearded man was filling buckets with fresh flowers, his work apron covering his worn, woolen clothing.

"May I help you?" he asked, wiping his hands on the apron.

"I'd like to buy some flowers," Edmund said, which, Felicity thought, was painfully obvious. Why else would one enter a flower shop?

Felicity was mindful of her wide hoop skirt as she passed vases and buckets of flowers, careful not to knock anything over. She inspected the blossoms. Some of the flowers were a bit wilted, but there were plenty of fresh ones to choose from.

"Might I recommend these yellow carnations?" the man asked. "They've just arrived."

Edmund raised an eyebrow at Felicity, who gave him a firm shake of her head.

"I think not," Edmund said. He pointed to a bucket of daisies and glanced at Felicity.

Felicity brushed past him and stopped by a bucket of brightly colored flowers with tightly layered petals. She pulled a small book from her *reticule. The Language of Flowers: An Alphabet of Floral Emblems* was newly published, and she was eager to put her copy to use. Felicity flipped through the pages comparing the entries with the flowers in the shop. She stopped by some pink, yellow, and white flowers. "Take a look at these, Edmund. A few of them, with a sprig of mint, would make an attractive nosegay and suit your purposes."

"Are you sure?" Edmund asked. "What was wrong with the carnations?"

"I thought you wanted her to like you," Felicity said. She thumbed through the book and pointed to a page. "Yellow carnations mean disdain, while the ranunculus means you think she is attractive."

"And the mint?"

"It shows the warmth of your feelings. This pairing will indicate your high opinion of her."

"Does it matter what color?" he asked.

"Not with the ranunculus."

"Where can I buy mint?"

"We have some in the garden at home. You choose the flowers you want, and I'll put the nosegay together for you," Felicity said. She wandered further into the shop, pausing by the bucket of yellow carnations. They were beautiful, and it was most unfortunate that a negative meaning was attached to them. But she would not let that stop her from getting some.

"Edmund! Get some of the yellow carnations, too," she said.

His brow wrinkled in confusion. "But you said...."

She pulled three carnations from the bucket and handed them to him. "Not for you," she said. "I'll pair them with some daisies and a rosebud from the garden and paint them. It'd be a shame for them to go to waste."

Edmund added the carnations to the ranunculus and gave them to the florist, who wrapped them in paper. Felicity, meanwhile, wandered to a back corner of the shop to examine some potted ferns.

The bell over the door jangled, and she glanced over to see two women entering the shop. Miss Sylvia Eggleton and Miss Emmaline Hyde. It was highly unlikely that she would be able to leave the shop without passing by them, and she would have to exchange pleasantries with them, although there had been many times Miss Eggleton was unpleasant in the past. With a sigh, she left the ferns and walked to the front of the shop.

"Good afternoon, Felicity," Emmaline said.

Sylvia scanned the shop as if to see who had accompanied Felicity there. When she spotted Edmund, she went over to him.

"Mr. Wixom, what a surprise to find you here! I see you have bought flowers. You must show them to me at once." Sylvia tried to open the paper-wrapped package, but Edmund moved it out of her reach.

"I'm afraid not, Miss Eggleton. They are to be a surprise."

Sylvia pouted. "I won't spoil anything if you let me see them."

Felicity excused herself from Emmaline and went to rescue her brother. "Edmund, we must be going."

"If you won't show them to me, at least tell me what you bought," Sylvia said, twirling a strand of hair around her finger and gazing up at Edmund.

Felicity rolled her eyes. "But what would be the surprise in that? You could easily identify Edmund to the flower's recipient." Her directness often made her unpopular with her peers, but Sylvia Eggleton's coaxing and flirting was trying her patience.

"Felicity is right, we must be going," Edmund said. "Good day, Miss Eggleton, Miss Hyde." They hurried out of the shop, and Felicity was relieved to enter the carriage and head for home.

"Miss Eggleton was quite...." Edmund paused, as if searching for the right word.

"Bold? Overbearing? Troublesome?" Felicity suggested.

Edmund chuckled. "All of those. I feared she would snatch the package right out of my hands."

"Like an overeager hound anticipating a treat," Felicity said. "Perhaps she is jealous."

"Jealous? Of what?" Edmund appeared perplexed.

"How can you be so oblivious? As soon as she saw me in the shop, she looked for you. And once she found you, she headed right over and started a conversation. And she wanted to see the flowers. The whole world can see she was trying to capture your interest, and she was quite dismayed when she failed."

Edmund grinned at her. "How do you do that? You always seem to know what is going on with people."

"How can you *not* notice? It's as if you wear blinders when it comes to the opposite sex. Except one woman has somehow managed to draw your attention." She glanced meaningfully at the flowers.

"You are curious, aren't you?" Edmund said.

She shook her head. "Care killed the cat. You'll tell me when you are ready."

"That's why Silas and I made you one of the three musketeers," Edmund said.

"Speaking of the three of us, have you heard from Silas?" Felicity asked.

Edmund shook his head. "Not since that letter weeks ago."

Felicity sighed. The time it took for letters to travel back and forth to India was truly frustrating. By the time one arrived, everything in it was old news. She hated having their little group separated. Edmund was still here, but as Father had him assume more responsibility around the estate, he was less available. And she had no idea when, or even if, Silas would return from India. When he left, he told her he'd be gone for at least a year, maybe two. But it was also possible that he would find working in

India to his liking and not return at all. She pushed that thought away.

The carriage jolted as a wheel hit a rut. The flowers jounced off Edmund's lap and Felicity caught them before they tumbled to the floor. She handed them back to him, undamaged.

"You may not have the curiosity of a cat, but you have cat-like reflexes." Edmund grinned at her.

When they arrived at Ashwick Manor, Felicity was the first to leave the carriage. "Put those flowers in water in the scullery. I'll find a bit of ribbon and get some mint. You must send them today."

"Do I send a note with them?" Edmund asked.

"Yes," Felicity said, exasperated. For a twenty-five-year-old man planning to run an estate, he required a surprising amount of guidance.

"What should I write? *Your blue dress is most flattering. I must see you. From your most ardent admirer*?" he asked.

Felicity's eyes widened in alarm. "Don't write that! You must be more subtle. Perhaps something about sending her this little bouquet to wish her a delightful day."

"That's it? No hint that I wish to court her?"

"If you wish to disregard my advice, try it your way and see what happens. Surely this time will be different because you wish it to be so."

"You make a fair point. I shall send a note as you suggest. How will I know its effect?"

Felicity placed her hand on his arm. "I have a strategy for you to follow. Later, you'll send her a single flower with a note revealing your identity. I think you'll soon be invited to visit. And if notes and flowers do not work, remember that you have tolerable good looks, and on occasion, you make coherent conversation. Even if she thinks you are a complete imbecile, you are the heir to Ashwick Manor, and that will be enough to make up for any of your shortcomings."

Edmund gave her a wry smile. "You are so good at keeping me humble."

"What are sisters for?" she said and headed to the garden to fetch a sprig of mint.

Chapter Four

May 15, 1857

Flagstaff Tower, India

A trickle of refugees made their way to Flagstaff Tower in small groups over the next few days. Silas listened to their stories of narrow escapes and of the violence they had witnessed. His anxiety over Mr. Talbot's safety grew. Mrs. Talbot and her children spent most of the time in the cramped tower room, but there was not enough space for everybody. Silas estimated the circular room held a hundred people, less if they wanted to sit or try to sleep. He didn't know how they could remain in such unbearably hot quarters during the day. A few had come out to get some air.

He paced back and forth in front of the tower under the warm afternoon sun and gazed toward Delhi. To his surprise, he saw a cloud of dust moving up the ridge that could only indicate a large group of people were coming. Whether friend or foe, he couldn't tell. He went immediately to tell the Brigadier.

"Someone is coming," he said, gesturing at the dust on the ridge.

"Have the men stand guard in front of the tower door. Keep the women and children inside until we know who it is."

Silas helped usher the women and children to safety while the servants gathered with the men outside the tower door in a protective stance. As the men reached the top of the ridge, Silas recognized they were sepoys, the native soldiers serving the East India Company. If this group decided to attack, they would all be easy targets. His insides quavered and he longed to run, but he would not desert Mrs. Talbot.

The captain of the group, a British man, stepped forward. "I am Captain Tytler of the 38th Infantry. We've come to help. We will escort everyone to Karnal, and I suggest we leave immediately, if you give the order, Sir."

Relief washed over Silas. They were no longer alone.

But the Brigadier was skeptical. "How do I know your men won't lure us away from the tower and attack?"

"I understand your concern, but these men are the very best I have. They have all pledged their loyalty to me, and I trust them. With all due respect, Sir, we need to see to the safety of the women and children."

A loud boom filled the air and the ground shook, reverberating through the earth with a low rumble. The children shrieked and clung to their mother's skirts as a thick plume of black smoke rose over Delhi. The Brigadier's hand instinctively reached for his weapon even as blood drained from his face.

"What is it?" Silas asked.

The man shook his head, staring at the horizon in dismay. He ran a hand over his forehead as if he could wipe away what he was seeing.

When he got no response from the Brigadier, Silas turned to Captain Tytler. "That sound, the shaking. What's happened?"

Captain Tytler pointed to the smoke plume. "They've blown up the munitions."

Mrs. Talbot joined them. "Who has done it? The rebels?"

The captain shook his head. "No, I think we did it."

"Why?" she asked.

"When you have lost the battle, you don't want to arm your enemies as you retreat." Captain Tytler turned to the Brigadier. "Sir, we must leave as soon as possible."

The older gentleman nodded. "Yes, please see to it, Captain."

Captain Tytler shouted orders to his men who sprang into action.

It was hard for Silas to comprehend what was happening around him. The ground was shaky beneath his feet, not because the tremors continued, but because the world no longer seemed stable. Everything was changing so rapidly.

"Mr. Parker, what does it mean?" Mrs. Talbot asked.

Her eyes were filled with fear, and he hated to add to all the uncertainty. But they could not move forward until they faced what was happening. "It means Delhi has fallen. The mutineers are in charge."

She gasped and rushed toward the tower. "Charlie! Hannah!"

Silas followed after her. "Make sure you have all of your belongings. I'll find a cart for you and the children."

She waved a hand at him in acknowledgement as she hurried inside the tower. Silas rushed over to the carts. A lone wagon pulled by a team of oxen approached. A grizzled man walked beside the oxen, prodding them forward. The wagon was good-sized and would hold several people, but it was not empty. Silas went to take a closer look and immediately wished he hadn't. The wagon was filled with bodies.

"Who are they? Where did they come from?" Silas asked in shock.

"Main Guard," the old man said.

Silas's stomach lurched. What if Mr. Talbot had gone to the Main Guard? Could he be here on this cart? Bile burned his throat at the thought of making a close examination of the cargo.

"Who told you to bring this here?" Captain Tytler confronted the man. "This wagon should have gone to Meerut, not here to the tower."

The man said something, but Silas did not hear. He inched closer to the cart. Flies buzzed around his head as he tried to make sense of the twisted skirts, limp hands, and pale faces. One woman's eyes were open, dull and dead, staring at him.

"Move away," Captain Tytler said. "There is no need for you to be here."

"I have to know if Charles Talbot is on that cart," Silas said.

"I'll help you." Captain Tytler called to two of his men who dashed over to assist. They shifted bodies so Silas could see all the faces. Faces that would be forever entrenched in his mind. He tried to ignore their wounds and their horrified expressions. Much to his relief, they did not find Mr. Talbot.

Captain Tytler spoke to the man who turned the oxen around and started down the ridge. Silas's vision clouded black and a ringing filled his ears. Hands guided him to a boulder and pushed down on his shoulders until he sat.

"Bend over, man," Captain Tytler said. "And take deep breaths. You'll be all right. Even soldiers have a hard time with the casualties of war."

Silas did as he was told. When he no longer feared he would faint, he made his way over to the Talbot family.

"Where were you?" Hannah asked, clutching her doll.

"I had to check on something, but I'm here now. Have you found a cart to ride in?"

Charlie pointed to one nearby. "Yes. Are you riding with us?"

Silas shook his head. "I'll leave the seat for someone else."

The sun was setting, and a light breeze stirred the air. "You must join us, Mr. Parker," Mrs. Talbot said.

He pulled her aside. "I think I should go back to Delhi. I may be able to find news about Mr. Talbot."

Her eyes widened in alarm. "You will do no such thing. Charles would want you to stay safe and to look after us."

Captain Tytler called for the carts to move forward. Mrs. Talbot hurried aboard, sitting between Hannah and Charlie with the valise on her lap. Charlie held the food basket.

"Will we be safe traveling at night?" she called to him.

"Yes," Silas said. "We have the infantry with us, and the moon is bright. I think you need to get as far away from Delhi as you can."

"We, Mr. Parker. We all need to get away from Delhi. Promise me you are coming with us."

It would be easy to turn the responsibility for the Talbots over to the infantry and to declare his own part in it finished. But if the tables were turned, if Silas were the one separated from a family, and Mr. Talbot were here, he knew what Charles would do.

"I promise," Silas said.

Hours passed as he trudged alongside the Talbot's cart, until his feet were sore, unused to so much walking. He thought he would collapse with fatigue. The group finally stopped near a grove of trees outside a small village. The infantry planned to stand guard in shifts because, although the village was quiet, no one knew how far the rebellion had spread or what their welcome would be.

The women got the children settled, and Silas sat on a large boulder just beyond the trees. Mrs. Talbot came toward him, carrying the basket of food they'd brought from Delhi. It seemed like a lifetime ago that he'd stood in her kitchen while the servants packed it for them. He doubted much food remained.

"Have you eaten anything?" she asked.

Silas shook his head. Mrs. Talbot spread a napkin on the boulder between them and took out what remained of the chutney and bread. She set out a candle and lit it. "Have something. The children are already fast asleep."

It took most of his remaining energy to break off pieces of bread and lift them to his mouth. Still, after the long day, the food tasted like a bit of heaven.

"How far is it to Karnal?" Mrs. Talbot asked.

"It might take us all week to get there."

"The women are whispering about a wagon filled with bodies back at Flagstaff Tower," Mrs. Talbot said. "Do you know anything about it?"

Silas swallowed, the mouthful of bread sticking in his throat. He coughed to clear it. "Rest assured that Mr. Talbot was not on that wagon. I checked it myself," he said.

Her relief was visible. "Thank you, Mr. Parker. Do you think he may have escaped?"

"Indeed. Your husband treats everyone so well, I suspect that there are plenty of people in Delhi who would shelter him or help him get out."

She gazed up at the sky. "If anything has happened to Charles," she began.

"You must not think about that," Silas said. "You must hope that he is safe."

"I will continue to hope, Mr. Parker, but I must also plan for the welfare of my children. If something has happened to him, would you accompany us back to England?"

"I will, but I don't think it will come to that," Silas said. "You will be reunited with Mr. Talbot soon."

Mrs. Talbot sighed. "Tell me something that will get my mind off of all of this."

The memories of the day were not pleasant, and Silas wracked his brain for something else he could share. He remembered the letter from Felicity that he had tucked into his waistcoat days ago.

"I received a letter from England, and I haven't had a chance to read it."

"Who is it from?"

"Miss Felicity Wixom," he replied.

"Is she a relative or a romantic interest?" Mrs. Talbot asked.

Silas shook his head. "Neither. She is the younger sister of my good friend, Edmund. We've known each other for years."

"Read it," Mrs. Talbot urged.

He opened the seal, and tiny blue flowers fell to the ground. Mrs. Talbot picked them up and handed them to him. "Forget-me-nots. Is she sentimental?"

"The forget-me-nots are connected to our childhood," he said. "Nothing more."

She raised an eyebrow. "If you insist, Mr. Parker. But tell me, how many other young ladies are pressing flowers and sending them all the way from England?"

"She's like a sister to me," Silas muttered as he opened the letter, squinting at it in the dim light. But, if he had only brotherly feelings towards her, why did he look forward to her letters with such anticipation? Felicity crossed his mind lately far more than he'd like to admit. Perhaps absence did truly make the heart grow fonder.

He skimmed the contents of the letter.

Dear Silas,

I hope this letter finds you well. Honestly, I hope this letter somehow finds you. India seems so very far away.

I will have a big surprise to show you when you return home. I hope Edmund will not spoil it and tell you. But then, I do not believe he is inclined to write to you at length, so my secret may be safe.

Do write and tell me what plants you are seeing in India. Since it is unlikely I will ever travel there, you shall have to be my eyes.

What do you do to pass the time? Are there balls? Musicales? Have you taken up cricket?

Your mother has invited us to a garden party to celebrate May Day, and if the weather is pleasant, I have been told there shall be a game of croquet. Lucy has claimed Edmund for her partner, and I fear I shall be paired with your brother, John. He has become so dull now that he is a clergyman. I don't recall him ever being such a stick-in-the-mud until recently. If you were here to be my partner, I think we would easily win, but my chances are not as good without you. You know I am not the most skilled player.

It is strange to think that by the time this reaches you, the game will already be over, and you will be left to wonder who won.

After I failed to make a match this past season, Mother despairs that I shall never find a husband. I told her I plan to make myself so valuable to Edmund that I will be a doting aunt to his offspring, and he will allow me to live at Ashwick Manor forever. Mother failed to see any humor in my remarks, even when I told her it was all dependent upon Edmund succeeding in getting married, of course.

I am sending you a little piece of home, something I pressed from the garden last spring. By the time this letter reaches you, my forget-me-nots will be in bloom again. You know why they remind me of you.

Ever your friend,

Felicity

He read the letter to Mrs. Talbot before carefully refolding it and tucking it back into his waistcoat. Hearing from Felicity had transported him back to England. How he longed for home.

"What do the forget-me-nots mean?" Mrs. Talbot asked.

"When we were children, her family came to dinner. My mother had a potted orange plant, and Felicity stood on a chair to smell the blossoms. Edmund and I were chasing around, and we knocked her over. She cried, and our mothers came to see what was wrong. When they asked what happened, Felicity did not tell on us. We would have been in so much trouble, but she said she fell, and even when pressed, she would not change her story. Edmund and I declared her one of the three musketeers with us, and that night, before she left, I gave her some forget-me-nots as a token of our friendship."

"She sounds lovely," Mrs. Talbot said. "Perhaps when all of this is over, you will return to England and see where the friendship leads. There are worse things to build a relationship on."

"Felicity is worthy of more than I can offer her," Silas said. The Wixoms had never made him feel anything but welcome in their home, but he had never considered courting her for many reasons, the first being that she was Edmund's sister. But beyond that, he wanted so much more for her than he would ever be able to provide: a fine home and a beautiful garden with servants to tend it. He feared his position in society would not garner her the respect she deserved.

"Does she require a fortune?" Mrs. Talbot asked.

"It isn't that," Silas said. "Everyone in my family has a place. My oldest brother will inherit, the next has a military commission, and one has gone into the clergy, and I thought my place would be here, but now I don't know where I belong."

Before he came to India, Father had talked to him about becoming a solicitor and living a quiet life in Upper Pangford. Or in London if he was enamored with the city. At the time, he'd wanted to be out from under his father's scrutiny, and he thought being a clerk in India would give him steady work and a change of scenery. Now, however, he wanted the safety of England. And someone to share it with.

It was frustrating how their birth order determined their roles, and he believed he was destined to be the family disappointment. He had hoped the East India Company would be the answer, but now he knew that being here was turning out to be far more adventure than he'd ever wanted.

"I am fortunate that you are the fourth son, or you would not have been here to rescue us," Mrs. Talbot said.

The idea that being a fourth son was fortunate had never occurred to Silas. "Anyone would have done the same," he said.

Mrs. Talbot rose to her feet, brushed off her skirts, and packed up the remnants of their food. "I think you underestimate yourself, Mr. Parker. Not every man would have done what you did for us. And I think you should consider that Miss Wixom not only wrote to you, but she also sent you forget-me-nots. Trust me, Mr. Parker, that means something. Goodnight."

Silas lingered on the rock alone. Moonlight illuminated their makeshift camp, and it was of some comfort to him that the moon was constant. It shone over England as well as India.

He found a spot near the other men and stretched out to sleep. What Mrs. Talbot said lingered in his mind. Felicity had been there in the background of his life for so many years that he could not imagine her not being there. If his feelings for her changed, and hers did not, he would lose their friendship. He wasn't sure what he would do with his life now, but he knew one thing for certain. He would not do anything that would put his friendship with Felicity at risk.

Chapter Five

May 22, 1857

Karnal, India

Mrs. Talbot stood outside the house where she and her children planned to stay now that they'd all arrived safely in Karnal. Silas faced her, the silence between them suddenly awkward after days of traveling together. He had already said goodbye to Charlie and Hannah, who had been whisked away by a maid for baths, milk, and bread before bed. Now he must say goodbye to Mrs. Talbot and be on his way to the bungalow where he was staying with some of the other men until he could arrange passage home. There was no point in drawing out their goodbyes.

Mrs. Talbot cleared her throat. "I have decided to remain here in Karnal until I know what happened to my husband, so I will not need you to accompany me and the children back to England. But please allow me to give you something to repay your kindness to us."

Silas shook his head. "There is no need, Mrs. Talbot. It was a pleasure to work for your husband, and I hope he is able to join you soon."

Her eyes twinkled. "Wait here. I know just the thing." She hurried into the house and Silas stood outside, keenly aware that he needed a bath and a change of clothes. The only possession he'd brought with him from Delhi was Felicity's letter. His books and clothes were all lost to him now. He wondered if the personal belongings he'd left in England were still safe in his room. Tucked in a small box in one of his drawers were the Valentines Felicity sent him over the years. The first ones had childish handwriting and crooked lace, but the later ones were beautiful: hand-painted with delicate lettering, dried flowers, and bits of ribbon.

He hadn't received a Valentine from her this year, and he'd wondered about that. She'd always sent one in the past. But perhaps it was just as well that he hadn't gotten one because it would only be lost to him now, left behind in Delhi with his other possessions.

Mrs. Talbot reappeared and handed him a bright-colored paisley shawl. "It's cashmere," she said.

His rough fingers caught on the delicate fabric. "It's beautiful, but what will I do with a lady's shawl? Wouldn't it be better to save it for Hannah?"

She smiled at him. "When we were in Delhi and I was gathering things for us to take, I packed this shawl. It seems silly now, and yet, I carried it all the way here. Now I know its purpose. You must take it with you back to England and give it to your young lady."

"My young lady?"

"Felicity. She sent you forget-me-nots, you should give her this."

The shawl was a bigger gift than he had ever given her, and it could easily be mistaken for a token of courtship. "But it is not like that between us," Silas protested.

"Not yet," Mrs. Talbot said.

"I don't know if I dare give it to her. Or if I want to," he confessed. When he first arrived in India, he'd missed Felicity, and had entertained the thought of courting her. But he'd pushed those thoughts aside and focused on his work. Now, the thought of going home, of seeing her again, made his insides quiver like a molded jelly at a dinner party.

Mrs. Talbot tilted her head to one side. "We don't often get the chance to make a fresh start in life, Mr. Parker. You should make the most of it. Please let me know what happens." She stood on tiptoe and placed a light kiss on his cheek before going into the house.

Silas walked to the bungalow, shawl in hand. Karnal was calm and peaceful, far enough away from the rebellion that he could leave the tension of the journey behind him.

When he arrived at the bungalow, he found a bath, clean clothes, and a hot meal waiting for him. The water was heavenly after so many days on the road. He scrubbed his skin and washed his hair twice until the water was filthy. The gash on his head was healing slowly, and he took care to protect the wound.

Clean, fed, and tired, he went to bed early, but sleep failed to come. Every time he closed his eyes, he heard shouting in the streets and the sound of gunshots. His mind filled with the smell of smoke and the sensation of rocks hitting his body. Heart pounding, he climbed from the bed and paced the room. He peered out the window where the moon, no longer full, was still bright enough to illuminate the vacant street. Everything was still. The only sound was the hum of insects outside.

If he were home in Upper Pangford, he would slip out of the house, walk down to the river, and let the cool air calm the thoughts darting through his mind like tiny trout in a pool in springtime. The shawl from Mrs. Talbot sat on the chair beside his bed. He touched the silky fabric and wondered if Felicity would like it. The bright red shapes on the orange background reminded him of her summer flower garden.

He'd been afraid in Delhi, more afraid than he'd ever been before in his life, and he didn't want fear to govern him moving forward. Mrs. Talbot was right. It was time for a fresh start. He would write to Felicity and tell her that she was never far from his thoughts, and that he was interested in courting her. The thought made his palms sweat, but he wiped them on his nightshirt. He lit a candle and, by its flickering light, made his way to the parlor. Lifting the desktop, he found paper, pen, and ink, and he set to work.

Dear Fliss,

You have no idea how much comfort your letters have brought me these past few months. By the time you get this, you will no doubt have heard about the mutiny that is taking place. I have escaped the city and am safe for now. It has been the most challenging week of my life. I won't waste paper and ink describing my experiences here. Suffice it to say I have seen unspeakable things, and those things have changed what I want. I hope these changes are for the better.

Thank you for the forget-me-nots. I can't decide if you sent them to me because you were thinking of me, or if you wanted to remind me how you saved me from a stern reprimand the night Edmund and I made you fall. We thought Mother's orange tree was so exotic, and I don't blame you for wanting to smell the blossoms. Edmund and I were chasing around like wild things when we knocked you off the chair. I can only imagine how much your knees and elbow hurt.

I do not know why you didn't tell anyone we were at fault. You gazed up at me with your tear-filled blue eyes and insisted that you fell without any involvement from us. Forget-me-nots always remind me of your loyalty. After all these years, I understand what a treasure a true friend is.

Silas paused, caught up in memories of the way she raced after him and Edmund as a child, of her nervous smile as they grew older, and the softness of her hand when he danced with her for the first time. He loved her teasing laughter.

His mind jumped to the many things he needed to sort out tomorrow, including getting clothing of his own, and figuring out how to make his way out of India and back to England. But first, he wanted to finish the letter tonight while the other men slept. He filled another page before he was too tired to continue. He closed the desk and carried the candle back to his room. As he snuffed out the candle, he heard the other men snoring. He got in the bed and for the first time in well over a week, he fell into a deep, dreamless sleep.

Chapter Six

June 30, 1857

Upper Pangford, England

When Felicity arrived in the breakfast room, she found two cards waiting for her in the morning post. She stole a glance at Father, wondering if he had noticed one was from the Society of Female Artists. She had not gotten into their art show, and could not fathom why they were contacting her now. The other letter, a bit torn and battered, was from India. She eagerly broke the seal. Word from Silas at last. The letter was dated April 15th. It had taken over two months to reach her, and she was frustrated by the delay.

Dear Fliss,

We are relocating to Delhi, and I shall remain there for the rest of my time in India. Mr. Talbot has been assigned there by the East India Company, and I am his dutiful clerk. I am unaccustomed to the way the Company functions as if it represents the government here. The Company even trains its own military of native sepoys and sowars under British command. I suppose it is the way it has been for decades, but I find it all rather uncomfortable.

At least Mr. Talbot treats all of the people who work for him well. I try to model my behavior after his fine example. I am eager to see Delhi, but I don't know when I shall be able to get a letter to you. Please write to me and let me know what is happening in Upper Pangford. Edmund is hopeless as a correspondent.

Ever your friend,

Silas

Felicity folded the letter and set it near her plate. Silas had not mentioned the Valentine she'd sent him this year. Did that mean he no longer cared to receive them? She couldn't read his thoughts from so far away. She'd sent Valentines to him ever since she was eight years old, and, for this particular card, she'd copied a line from Shakespeare and embellished it with bits of lace and ribbon. Had her message been too forward? It was disappointing that he had not acknowledged receiving it and she wondered if it had gotten lost.

"Why is the Society of Female Artists sending you mail?" Father asked. His voice was stern.

"I don't know," Felicity said, truthfully. "I haven't opened it yet."

"Do so now." Father pushed his empty plate aside as she broke the seal.

"Well?" he asked.

Edmund had stopped eating, his eyes fixed on her.

She cleared her throat.

Dear Miss Wixom,

Our first art show was a great success, and we appreciate all who entered their work. While, as you know, your painting was not accepted, we at the Society of Female Artists believe your work shows great promise, and we invite you to apply to our art school. Please send a letter as your application. We encourage you to continue to paint, and to enter our exhibition next year.

Mrs. Harriet Newcombe

Society of Female Artists

Oxford Street, London

"You entered an exhibition after I forbade it?" Father asked.

"Forgive me, Father, but you told me I mustn't apply to art school. You said nothing about the exhibition."

He glared at her, and Felicity dropped her gaze to her plate. She didn't want him to be angry with her, and while technically she was correct, she had kept her entry a secret, knowing he would not approve.

"While you live in my house, you will not submit paintings for exhibition or apply to art school. It is unseemly for a woman of your status. Have I made myself clear?"

Felicity nodded. "Yes, Father." While she'd been disappointed that her art had not been accepted in the exhibition, it only reinforced her desire to improve. However, it would not do to go against Father's wishes and apply to art school. She would have to find some other way. To her relief, Father returned to his newspaper.

Edmund caught her eye. "I have followed your advice in my courtship and have sent the flowers and notes as you suggested. What is the next step I should take?"

"Send her one more flower with a note identifying yourself and see if you receive an invitation to call on her," Felicity said.

Father straightened in his chair. Frown lines wrinkled his forehead, and Felicity wondered what he was reading that made his demeanor change.

"I'm afraid there is some troubling news." He folded the newspaper to display a particular article and place it in front of Edmund.

Felicity tried to read it across the table, but she could not make out the headline.

"There has been an uprising in India," Edmund said, handing the paper to her.

Felicity skimmed the article, then reread it more slowly. "This tells us absolutely nothing," she said.

"Isn't Silas in Bombay? Or Calcutta?" Edmund asked.

Felicity shook her head. "The letter that arrived this morning said he was going to Delhi. He may have been there for over a month now." She'd never lamented the painfully slow communication with India as much as she did today. She fingered her fork, no longer having a desire to eat anything.

"I am certain young Mr. Parker is fine," Father said.

"You cannot be sure he is fine," Felicity said. "This rebellion or riot or whatever it is has most certainly made it to Delhi from Meerut for it is only twenty miles away!"

"How do you know that?" Edmund eyed her curiously.

"I may have looked at some maps," she said, not wanting to admit that she'd pored over them in Father's study so often since Silas left that she had a firm grasp of Indian geography. It made her worry less about him if she could envision where he was.

"Silas could be wounded, or...." She couldn't say it. He had to be alive. She refused to believe otherwise.

"You know Silas is very good at getting out of scrapes," Edmund said.

"Only when someone else is there to assist," she retorted, her mind flashing to the many times she had covered for Silas and Edmund and kept them out of trouble.

"Eat your breakfast," Father said. "Starving yourself will not help Mr. Parker, nor will it help you."

She poked her kedgeree with her fork. Today the mixture of smoked fish, seasoned rice, hard-boiled eggs, and butter had congealed into an unappealing mass on her plate. She would never be able to swallow even one bite of it. She bit into a piece of bread, hoping that it would calm the jitters in her stomach, but it was dry and tasteless in her mouth. She washed it down with some tea.

Edmund was having no problem eating his breakfast, and he glanced at the sideboard as if planning to get more.

Felicity got to her feet, reached across the table, and yanked Edmund's fork out of his hand. "How can you sit there and eat? Silas is your best friend!"

Lucy and Mother entered the room. Mother shook her head at Felicity. "It's too early for you to be bothering your brother, dear. The day is yet young."

Edmund grabbed her wrist and retrieved his fork. "Me worrying about Silas will not change a thing. This happened weeks ago, Fliss. It is likely the rebellion has passed and that he is safe and sound."

"I would like to call on the Parkers," Felicity said. "Perhaps they have had some word."

"Aren't you helping Louisa get ready for the garden party today?" Mother brought her tea and bread to the table. "We may call on Mrs. Parker tomorrow."

Felicity groaned at the reminder of the garden party. Louisa was her closest friend, but she dreaded an afternoon of conversations about hair ribbons and summer balls.

"May I come early and help you, Felicity?" Lucy's eyes were bright with hope. Felicity knew how much Lucy wanted to fully participate in Upper Pangford society this summer, but today she was in no mood to listen to Lucy's chatter while she helped Louisa.

"Not this time," she said. "I think it's best if you arrive with Mother." She set her napkin on the table. "Please excuse me. I need to gather a few things before I leave."

"You've hardly eaten a thing," Father said, frowning at her plate.

"Your eyes must be bigger than your belly," Edmund teased.

"I am afraid the news has robbed me of my appetite," she said.

"Perhaps you are too sensitive to read the paper," Edmund replied.

"You are impossible. Here," she handed him her plate. "Make yourself useful. We wouldn't want the food to go to waste." With that, she headed for her bedroom.

Felicity longed to write to Silas, but right now, she had to get out of the house. Maybe the walk to Louisa's would soothe her frayed nerves. She collected gloves and an apron and secured her hat to her head. Avoiding anyone in the house, she hurried down the stairs and out the door, escaping to the fresh morning air.

Silas had to come back. He just had to. He was always the one who was thoughtful...hoisting her up into the tree when she wasn't tall enough to follow him and Edmund, saving her a bit of apple tart when Edmund had eaten the last one, not laughing at her drawings. She did not want to think about a life without him in it.

She walked briskly down the drive, and when she was out of sight of the house, she broke into a run. It wasn't something she did often, but today, each footfall on the road and each deep exhale of air from her lungs released some of the worry from her body. Maybe Silas had gotten word in Delhi about the events in Meerut and had escaped to safety.

Edmund was right. All the worry in the world would not help Silas. She ran to the crossroads and then slowed to a walk, not caring that her face must be flushed from the exertion. By the time she reached the James's house, her breathing had returned to normal.

Felicity added a sprig of jasmine to the blue forget-me-nots and orange zinnias in the little vase. The flower arrangement still needed something. Louisa entered the room carrying a basket of ivy. "The gardener suggested this as greenery," she said, placing the ivy on Felicity's worktable. "We won't send a wrong message if we include it, will we?"

"I don't think so, but I'll check." Felicity thumbed through *The Language of Flowers.* While she'd only had her copy for a couple of months, it was already well-worn. "No, the ivy will be perfect."

She added the greenery to each of the bouquets, four in all. They would be lovely on the tables at the garden party. Felicity held up one for Louisa to inspect.

"Oh, Felicity, it's lovely. You have a gift with flowers! What do they all mean?"

"Ivy is for attachment, jasmine for amiability, and zinnias for everlasting friendship. The forget-me-nots are self-explanatory."

Louisa smiled in delight, her naturally rosy cheeks a perfect complement to her blue eyes and golden hair. "Mother will be so pleased. Thank you for your help."

"Who else is coming?" Felicity asked. She hoped Miss Eggleton was not on the guest list. Felicity doubted she could muster the energy to be polite to her today. Ever since they were newly out in society, Miss Eggleton had persisted in making derogatory remarks about her appearance or her behavior. She once said she doubted Felicity would ever convince a man to marry her.

It had been hurtful at the time, but with each passing year, Felicity worried less about someone else's opinion. Besides, Miss Eggleton did not have a suitor or a proposal of marriage either.

"The Turners are coming. They're new in the neighborhood. And they're bringing a guest. And of course, your mother and Lucy will be there, too." Louisa picked up two vases and gestured for Felicity to follow her.

"Have you heard about the skirmish in India?" Louisa asked.

Startled, Felicity dropped a vase. It hit the flagstones and shattered, spilling water and flowers. "I'm so sorry," Felicity said. She stooped to clean up the mess, but Louisa stopped her.

"It's nothing. I'll have someone come clean this up, and there are still some flowers and another vase inside. We can fix this." Louisa took her hand.

Felicity struggled to maintain her composure. "I found out about it this morning. Silas is in India, and I don't know if he is safe." Her throat burned.

Louisa squeezed Felicity's hands. "Don't lose hope. You may hear soon that it was all nothing and he is safe and sound. Cheer up, I'll have you sit with Mrs. Dalrymple during lunch."

Felicity sighed. "How will that help?"

Louisa gave her a reassuring smile. "I believe Mrs. Dalrymple will be the distraction you need this afternoon. Now dry your eyes and try not to worry."

When the guests arrived, Mrs. James introduced Felicity to Beatrice Turner, Mrs. Turner, and Mrs. Turner's sister, Mrs. Dalrymple.

"It's Miss Dalrymple," the woman corrected. "I have never married." Her brown hair was sprinkled with gray, and her cheerful face had wrinkles around her eyes that deepened when she smiled.

Felicity was seated, as Louisa promised, by Miss Dalrymple and her niece, Beatrice. Beatrice wore a deep purple dress that set off her dark hair and porcelain complexion. "May I call you Felicity?" Her tone was warm and her eyes were sincere.

"Yes, if I may call you Beatrice."

Beatrice agreed. "I do hope we shall become good friends."

"Tell me," Felicity said. "How do you occupy your time?"

"I did quite a bit of charity work in London. Are there opportunities for such work here in Upper Pangford?"

"Yes, there is a ladies' group that assists women and children in need. They would love to have you, I'm sure," Felicity replied.

Miss Dalrymple joined the conversation. "Beatrice is her happiest helping others or being outdoors with her horse. Miss James tells me we may have a common interest. I am a botanist."

That is why Louisa wanted them to sit together. Felicity was intrigued. She hadn't met a female scientist before. "I have an interest in flowers, but I am no botanist. I do enjoy drawing and painting them."

"An artist!" Miss Dalrymple said. "It is fate that has brought us together. I need someone to draw and paint the plants I am researching."

Doubt flooded Felicity's mind. Her family thought she had no skill, and she'd been rejected by the Society of Female Artists summer show. Why had she said anything about art? It would have been perfectly acceptable to say she liked to work in her garden. Miss Dalrymple was in need of a skilled professional, not an amateur.

"Felicity's floral paintings are beautiful. She has the skill to draw and paint them most accurately, but she also has a unique artistry in her work," Louisa said.

Felicity wanted to kick her friend under the table.

"I would like to see your work," Miss Dalrymple said.

"I may disappoint you, Miss Dalrymple. I've had no formal training."

Miss Dalrymple waved her hand as if brushing off Felicity's concern. "It is more important that you have trained your eye for detail. May I call on you tomorrow afternoon? I'll bring Beatrice with me."

How refreshing it was to discuss something other than marriage prospects. Felicity found she was looking forward to meeting with Miss Dalrymple and Beatrice again.

Chapter Seven

September 4, 1857

Upper Pangford, England

It was a beautiful September day, and Felicity had spent much of it outside, tending her garden. But now she must take advantage of the late afternoon light to paint the orchid Miss Dalrymple had left in her care. The delicate white and pink blossoms arched over the deep green leaves and Felicity concentrated on capturing not only a likeness of it on the canvas, but also the feelings it evoked within her. It was delicate, but strong. Calm, yet courageous.

Miss Dalrymple was expecting new plant specimens from the West Indies: hibiscus, bromeliads, and a pitcher plant. Felicity was eager to paint them. Until then, she would be content with the orchid and the flowers she grew here at home.

The now-finished glass conservatory was warm and humid, and it reminded her of Silas's description of India. She wondered what plants he'd seen, but then her thoughts turned to worrying for his safety once again. She had not had any word from him since the mutiny began, and reports in the newspapers did nothing to allay her concerns.

As she painted, a tendril of hair curled against her damp cheek, and she brushed it aside. A blast of cool air rushed into the room, and she turned to see Edmund standing in the doorway.

"Mother sent me to fetch you for dinner," he said.

"Shut the door, Edmund. You'll let out all the warm air." She kept painting, determined to use up the batch of color on her palette before she abandoned the project for the day. "Tell Mother I will be there as soon as I use up this bit of paint."

Edmund peered over her shoulder. "She said I am not to leave the room without you, and I am in dire need of food. I shall perish if you don't come at once."

Felicity laughed. "Then I shall take my time, for if you perish, I will inherit Ashwick Manor and all of my troubles will be over."

Edmund thumped a fist against his heart. "You wound me, sister. How can you be so casual about my demise?" He tugged at the loose strand of her hair and let it fall across her cheek.

Felicity pushed his hand away and tucked the strand firmly behind her ear.

Edmund tapped his foot as he waited for her. It disturbed her concentration. At last, she gathered her brushes. "I'll take these to the scullery, and then I'll meet you in the dining room," she said.

Edmund's eyes twinkled at her. The mischievous grin on his face told her something was afoot.

"What are you not telling me?" she asked.

He shook his head. "Nothing, Fliss. It's time for dinner. That's all."

She raised an eyebrow, not trusting him one bit. "I've asked you time and again not to call me Fliss. Go on then, I'll be there in a minute."

He tapped the tip of her nose with his finger. "Do hurry."

She took her brushes to the scullery and hung her apron on a hook near the door. She scrubbed all but the most stubborn paint off her hands. She didn't have time to change out of her brown painting dress and to redo her hair when the others were waiting for her. Hopefully Mother would not reprimand her for her disheveled appearance.

When she reached the dining room, she found, to her surprise, that they had company. This was what Edmund had been keeping from her. She turned to run upstairs and change her stained dress, to brush her hair and pin it back up, but Mother called her.

"Felicity, there you are! We've been waiting for you. Please sit."

Reluctantly, she entered the room. The Parker family was seated at the long dining table with her family. John Parker sat next to Lucy, and Mr. and Mrs. Parker were seated near her parents. The only empty seat was across from Edmund next to Silas Parker.

Silas.

She gasped and her hands flew to her face. "Are you really here?"

His eyes locked on hers and he nodded. Tears of relief brimmed her eyes and spilled over on her cheeks.

For a moment, they were the only two people in the room. Dear, familiar, Silas was home safe and sound. He was thinner than she remembered, and a new scar made a line through his left eyebrow. But his wavy brown hair and warm hazel eyes were unchanged.

Under his steady gaze, she brushed away her tears. He rose from his chair, and she gathered her wits, urging her trembling feet and legs to carry her to the seat beside him.

Softly, so no one else could hear, she leaned toward him. "Are you well?"

He gave her a reassuring smile. "I am. And I am happy to be back home."

As the footmen brought the first course. Edmund grinned at her.

"Why didn't you say something?" she hissed.

He shrugged. "And miss this moment? Not a chance. But here we are, the three musketeers, reunited."

"At last," she said. She turned back to Silas, still struggling to believe he was really here beside her. "If I had known you were going to be here, I'd have changed my clothes and...."

He stopped her. "You are beautiful, Fliss. Don't fret over things that do not matter."

"When did you get back?"

"I arrived home yesterday," he said.

"You must be exhausted. Was the journey very tedious?" Felicity asked.

"Each day was agonizingly slow, but also a blessing because I was headed in the right direction. The journey could not go fast enough for me."

As the footman served dinner, Felicity kept her rough, paint-stained hands in her lap. She wished she'd had more time to scrub them clean, to rub something on to smooth her skin. If she hadn't been so engrossed in the painting, if Edmund had warned her that they had company, if she'd had a little more time, then she could have arrived at dinner in a clean dress with neatly coiffed hair.

She had never worried about what Silas thought of her appearance before, and she wondered at the change now. She had missed him terribly, but that was not enough to explain her sudden urge to look her best for him. Always before he had been a dear friend, but now it was as if she had butterfly wings tickling her insides, lifting her heart toward something more.

Silas nudged her arm with his elbow, the movement so slight she was certain no one else had noticed it. She glanced down to see him holding out a handkerchief. His hand was lower than the table height, and no one else could see. With his other hand, he touched his right cheek.

"You have a smudge," he said softly.

She accepted the handkerchief and dabbed at her cheek. He shook his head, indicating she had not removed the mark.

She scrubbed harder. Purple paint left a smear on the white fabric. Drat that Edmund. He'd known! He'd known she had paint on her cheek, and in all likelihood, in her hair. And he'd known Silas was here at dinner. She frowned at him, but he shrugged his shoulders, an innocent expression on his face.

Silas cleared his throat. "Much better," he said, holding out his hand.

She folded the handkerchief before handing it back to him. "Now you have something to remember me by," she said, indicating the paint stain.

His mouth twitched. "As if I could forget you." His fingers grazed hers as he took the handkerchief.

The touch sparked a desire in her to give him the most enormous hug, to wrap her arms around him and tell him how much she had worried these past few months with no word from him. To let him know how happy she was to see him. Instead, she pinched his arm.

"Ow!" he said. "Why did you do that?"

"You have been away so long without any word, I had to verify that you are not an apparition. But it seems you are truly here. Welcome home."

He rubbed his arm as if wounded. Felicity knew she had not pinched hard enough to cause him any harm through his sleeve.

"Have I appeared to you as an apparition before? Or haunted your dreams?" Silas tucked the handkerchief in a pocket and picked up his knife and fork.

"I don't dream about you," Felicity said, which was not quite the truth. Since she'd gotten word about the mutiny, she had dreamed of Silas exactly twice: once she dreamed he was in grave peril, and once that they were on a picnic together, safe and sound. She knew which dream she preferred, but she would never tell him about either of them.

"Have you had any gardening triumphs of late?" he asked, between bites of food.

Trust Silas to steer the conversation onto safe ground. She spread her napkin across her lap. "I have failed to convince my forget-me-nots to bloom indoors during the winter. Sadly, I shall have to wait for them to bloom this spring."

"It's a good thing you pressed some to send to me in India then. I was happy to receive them, knowing of your fondness for the plant."

"I am glad you received my letter, and you know I always remember the forget-me-nots you gave me after you and Edmund knocked me off that chair when we were having dinner at your house. They remind me I am one of the three musketeers with you."

"Your heroic actions kept us from being reprimanded, and I, for one, will never forget it," Silas said.

"Are you going back to India?"

"I will be staying in England."

"Then you won't be sending me letters, I suppose. Unless you plan to go to London?"

"I'd rather not," Silas said. "I believe it is time for me to move on from the East India Company, and I plan to complete my training as a solicitor here in Upper Pangford."

"How very practical of you," she said. "I imagine it will give you plenty of time to pursue mental flights of fancy while you work. Or you shall die of boredom." A footman cleared her plate and set the next course in front of her.

Silas dabbed his mouth with his napkin. "Practical is very appealing to me right now. I have had enough adventure to last a lifetime."

Whatever had happened to him in India had changed him. She wondered if his scars ran deeper than the one on his forehead, but she sensed his reluctance to say more. Still, if he ever wished to talk about it, she wanted him to know she was willing to listen.

"As your dearest friend, I expect that I shall be the first to hear the details of your adventures."

He stiffened beside her and his fork dropped to his plate with a clatter.

His experiences during the mutiny must be upsetting to him. Silas picked up his fork once again, and Felicity continued to speak as if nothing had happened. "Despite your long history with my brother, I know that Edmund cannot possibly be your dearest friend." Her strategy worked, and Silas grinned.

"He did not send me forget-me-nots, so no. I don't believe he qualifies."

Edmund protested from across the table, and Felicity was relieved to see Silas settling in with both of them once again.

"I, for one, am happy you are not returning to India or to London, and I am sure we will find things here to keep ourselves occupied. It has been very dull with only Edmund for company," Felicity said.

"That's not true," Edmund said, a little too loudly. Mother frowned at him, much to Felicity's delight.

To her surprise, Silas took her hand again beneath the table and gave it a squeeze, his thumb lightly rubbing her skin. She did not look at him, did not count the seconds that his touch lingered, did not contemplate the way his touch warmed her heart. Before she could respond, he removed his hand and joined the conversation with her father.

What did he mean by holding her hand in such a way? While she and Silas had always shared a level of familiarity with one another, this action was unexpected. Felicity decided not to dwell on it. He was glad to be home, that was all. And the important thing to her was that he was safe and in her life once again.

Chapter Eight

Upper Pangford, England

September 4, 1857

It had been an impulse to grab Felicity's hand. Silas hoped his face was not as inflamed as it felt. He shouldn't have done it. But she hadn't torn her hand away. His head was a muddle, and everything here in England, while familiar, was also rather strange to him. While it was tempting to fall back into old patterns, he did not want to. Mrs. Talbot was right. This fresh start was a gift, and he should make the most of it.

Seeing Felicity, however, made him doubt what had been so clear in his mind from the deck of a ship. Then, he pictured arriving home and meeting her someplace alone, like in her garden, and giving her the letter he'd written in India and confessing his feelings for her. Instead, here she was pinching his arm as if she were a mischievous younger sibling.

She was exactly how he remembered her with her light blue eyes and a smattering of freckles across her face, but she was also different. He couldn't put his finger on what had changed, but it only made her more attractive to him. Still, it was so easy to slip back into comfortable interactions with her and Edmund. Maybe he did not want to put that at risk.

When there was a lull in the conversation with Mr. Wixom, he turned his attention back to Felicity and Edmund.

"What have I missed while I've been away?"

Edmund's face twitched and he focused on his plate, not meeting Silas's gaze.

"Edmund is in love," Felicity said, calmly cutting a piece of meat and lifting it to her mouth.

"I am not!" Edmund frowned at her.

"I wouldn't say that so emphatically if I were you," Felicity replied. She turned her attention back to Silas. "Edmund is courting, and I have been advising him."

"That is news," Silas said. "Anyone I know?"

Edmund remained silent, but Felicity said, "Miss Evangeline Harris."

"Evangeline?"

"Don't act so surprised," Edmund said.

"I am happy for you. If I recall, Evangeline is younger than Fliss."

"She is two years younger than Felicity, but she is wise beyond her years," Edmund said.

"I don't know that I would call her wise, as she has fallen for your foolishness," Felicity teased. "But the two of you are a good pair."

"Why does Silas get to call you Fliss and I don't?" Edmund asked.

"While I have outgrown you calling me that, Silas gave me the nickname and therefore, he retains proprietary use." She winked at Silas and warmth filled him.

For the first time since his arrival in England he relaxed in their company, enjoying the conversation. It was a surprise that Edmund was earnestly courting someone, but now he wondered about Felicity. He hesitated to ask, not sure he would like the answer. But he needed to know.

He attempted to keep his tone light. "Have you found a match?"

Felicity dabbed her mouth with her napkin. "I have been far too busy assisting Edmund to worry about such nonsense for myself."

A smile played across his lips at her answer. If she was not being courted by anyone else, she might be open to finding out if they were a good fit for each other.

"Edmund is hopeless at understanding the language of flowers without my guidance," Felicity continued. "But because of my advice, he has been invited to call on Evangeline several times. If you are ever in need of my skills, I am happy to help."

"I'll keep that in mind," he said.

After dinner, the men followed the women to the drawing room, skipping the usual ritual of sharing a drink in the dining area. Silas spoke to a footman on the way out. The man nodded and left on his errand. He returned with a package.

Mrs. Parker frowned. Silas knew Mother would not approve of him giving a gift to Felicity. It was rather forward of him, but here, with their families, the gift was less intimate than if he presented it to her when they were alone. He took the package from the footman and gave it to her.

"For me?" she said in surprise.

"Your letters sustained me through a difficult time, and this is my way of expressing my gratitude," he said.

"You knew I would keep my promise to stay in contact," she said. "I even sent you a Valentine. Did you receive it?"

She *had* sent him one. That thought filled him with comfort. "I never got it, Fliss, much to my regret."

"I am sorry to hear it didn't arrive. I did not want to break our tradition."

It was gratifying to know she thought of the Valentines as their tradition. "Open your gift," he said, eager to see her reaction.

She tore the paper wrapping and revealed the shawl. The paisley design was a riot of oranges and reds, and she traced over the pattern with her finger. "It's beautiful."

"It's the color of your marigolds," Silas said. "Marigolds are all over India, and when I saw them, it reminded me of you. Put it on."

Felicity shook out the folds from the fabric and wrapped the shawl around her shoulders. It brought life to the simple brown dress she wore. Felicity should, in his opinion, always wear the bright colors of her flower garden.

Mrs. Parker cleared her throat. "Marigolds are for grief and despair. How could you make that comparison?"

He wrinkled his forehead and glanced from his mother to Felicity. "In India, they are used for celebrations."

"Then they are perfect for tonight, as we celebrate your return. But in England, you might also say the shawl is the color of zinnias, for absent friends," Felicity said.

Felicity was stepping in to save him from his mother once again. He gave her a warm smile. "I am no longer absent."

"For that, I am most grateful. I shall wear it often," she said.

"I hope so. It becomes you. Now, what is the surprise you wrote to me about?"

Felicity's face lit up. "Edmund didn't spoil it for you?"

"No, Edmund said nothing."

She set the shawl on a chair and gave him a mischievous grin. "Close your eyes."

He obeyed, and she took his arm and guided him across the room. He heard a door open and a wave of warm air wrapped around him. Felicity led him forward and he sensed her closing a door behind them. She released his arm. "Open your eyes."

He did as she asked and gazed in wonder at the glass conservatory filled with plants. It had not been there when he last visited the Wixom home. The warmth combined with the delicate scent of flowers reminded him of the best things in India.

Felicity spread her arms wide. "Isn't it wonderful? It was under construction all summer and I thought it would never be finished. It's my favorite place, and I daresay I shall never leave it."

"It's beautiful, Fliss," he said, wandering over near a potted orange tree like the one his mother once had.

"It's not the Crystal Palace."

"No. It's much more pleasing. Small enough to be cozy, and large enough to hold a gathering." Silas plucked an orange blossom and tucked it behind her ear, letting his finger trail down her cheek to her chin.

"Silas, I," she began.

"Yes?" He searched her eyes, sensing a new tension between them.

"I shall never be able to grow an orange if you pick the blossoms." Her voice was soft, her eyes focused on him.

He burst out laughing. He didn't remember the last time he laughed. It was not only coming home that was healing, but it was this: being back with his friends. Being with Felicity. For the first time since the mutiny, he had hope of moving past the difficult memories.

Lucy entered the conservatory, closing the door securely behind her. She reminded him of Felicity at that age, only with golden hair. She walked toward them, hands clasped behind her back, an impish grin on her face. "I see you have discovered Felicity's favorite place. Father has to give her an allowance, or she would bankrupt the estate buying plants."

"Money spent on plants is never wasted," Felicity said.

"Mother has sent me to chaperone you, and I see I have arrived just in time." Lucy pointed to the orange blossom in Felicity's hair. "Mr. Parker gave you a token of love. Everyone knows it is a marriage flower."

"Silas knows as much about the meaning of flowers as Edmund," Felicity said. "He gave it to me because he knows I enjoy them and for no other reason."

"If you say so," Lucy said with a grin.

Silas wandered further into the conservatory, Lucy trailing after him. Felicity stayed behind, examining the orange tree.

"She was worried about you while you were away," Lucy said.

"I am glad to be home to put her mind at ease."

Lucy raised her eyebrow at him. "If you do not have a romantic intent towards her, be careful of your actions. You may not have known the meaning of the orange blossom, but she did. And I don't want to see her hurt."

Silas straightened his shoulders and faced Lucy. "I have a very high opinion of your sister. She is, after all, one of us musketeers. It is not my intent to hurt her."

"Very well," Lucy said. "If you will excuse me, I believe Edmund is calling me."

Silas heard nothing, but Lucy slipped out of the conservatory, leaving him alone with Felicity. He wouldn't be surprised if she done it purposely.

Felicity joined him, the blossom still tucked behind her ear. He thought about saying something about the flower, of making some sort of jest about it, but he decided against it. The flower had been an impulse, but not a mistake.

"Did Lucy leave? She was not a very good chaperone," Felicity said.

Silas moved closer to her. "Or, perhaps she was the perfect chaperone."

Felicity's eyes shone. "Think of the mischief we could make with our families only a door away."

Her contentment showed in this place, and glancing around, he could see why she loved it. The variety of hues and textures in the plants evoked a sense of calm. He let his gaze wander over the high ceiling and down to the far corner of the room where he spied a canvas resting against the glass wall.

"What's this?" he said, pointing.

Felicity's cheeks flushed. "That? That's nothing."

Curious, he picked it up and turned it over, revealing a painting of forget-me-nots, the brushstrokes as delicate as the flowers themselves. It was stunning. He squinted at the signature on the bottom of the painting. *F. Wixom.* He remembered her early attempts at painting, none of them yielding something like this.

"I hope I won't offend you when I say I am impressed by how much you've improved. Why isn't it on a wall instead of hiding in the corner?" he asked.

"Unfortunately, not everyone shares your opinion, so for now, it lives here." She took the painting from him and returned it to the corner. A hint of sadness flashed across her face, and he wondered at the cause of it.

It was surprising that anyone could disapprove of her art, and he longed to ask her more. But, sensing she did not wish to discuss it tonight, and wary of Lucy's concern that he not hurt Felicity, he decided not to pursue the subject. If she wished him to know, she would tell him.

"Well, from one musketeer to another," he said, bowing with a flourish, "I believe it belongs in a place of honor. And I hope you paint more."

She smiled at him and dipped into a curtsey. "Why thank you, sir. I believe I shall."

Chapter Nine

September 18, 1857

Upper Pangford, England

Lucy gripped Felicity's arm, her excitement almost palpable. "Isn't it beautiful? I hope we dance every dance." Her face flushed a delicate pink, matching the color of her gown. Felicity had chosen a deep blue dress for the evening.

Hundreds of candles in wall sconces and chandeliers had, indeed, transformed the ordinary assembly rooms of Upper Pangford into an enchanted ballroom.

"It's lovely," Felicity said. "Even more so from up there, which is where I shall be if you need me." She pointed to the landing overlooking the ballroom.

"You won't get asked to dance if you are up there," Lucy said.

"Which makes it the very best vantage point."

"At least wait until I get asked. I can't face standing here all alone." Lucy linked her arm through Felicity's and they wound their way further into the room, joining Louisa James. Louisa's emerald green dress set off the golden highlights in her ringlets.

"You must convince Felicity to dance," Lucy said as Louisa greeted them.

"Yes, you must dance," Louisa said. "But first, tell me everything about Silas Parker."

Felicity scanned the room. "Is Silas here?"

"Over near the refreshments with your brother. He is more handsome than I remember," Louisa said.

Felicity hadn't seen him since the dinner at her house, and she was thrilled to see him now, handsome in his tailcoat. Tonight, he was the picture of health, the gaunt look gone from his face.

"Too bad he is in need of a fortune, or I would pursue him. He will be a good match for someone. I suspect all the eligible ladies will be after him tonight. What about you, Felicity? Have you any interest in him?" Louisa asked.

"I think Felicity has always been interested in him," Lucy said. "You should see the way they look at one another."

"Lucy!" Felicity tapped her sister on the arm with her fan.

"Are you surprised that I know?" Lucy asked.

"You are mistaken. Ignore everything she says," Felicity told Louisa.

"I hear terrible rumors about him." Louisa opened her fan and waved it gently in front of her face. "Do you think any of them are true?"

"What have you heard?" Felicity was not aware of the gossip circulating around town, and normally she would not ask, but if people were disparaging Silas, he had the right to know.

Louisa proceeded to list several, from the ridiculous to the sublime. Felicity scoffed at them all. "You know Upper Pangford. You shouldn't believe everything you hear."

Lucy sidled closer to Felicity. "Benjamin Hughes is coming this way. What should I do?"

Felicity glanced at her younger sister. What was it about the presence of a man that turned intelligent women into fools? "Hide!" Felicity said.

Lucy gasped. "Hide? Where?" Her eyes darted around the room as Benjamin came closer.

"Don't be a silly goose," Louisa said. "Your sister is teasing. If he asks you, and you wish to dance with him, accept the invitation."

Lucy gripped Felicity's hand. "Promise me you won't disappear while I am dancing."

"I promise," she said. How quickly it had gone by, her own debut in society, the thrill of balls and social engagements. Now it was routine, and all the events blended together in her head. She no longer wished to gossip about who danced with whom, to wonder what each gesture meant. Now, as Benjamin escorted Lucy to the dance floor, it was her sister's turn to revel in the novelty of it all.

Mr. Woodburn, a widower with a daughter Lucy's age, caught her eye and came toward her.

"Quick," Felicity said. "Mr. Woodburn is on the prowl." She grabbed Louisa's hand and led her into the crowd of people watching the couples dancing. Felicity hoped the man would not follow her.

Louisa looked behind them. "You are safe for now. He has found another partner."

"That was close. Thank you," Felicity said. She kept an eye on Lucy while she and Louisa talked.

"Have you been painting for Miss Dalrymple?" Louisa asked.

"I've been doing drawings for her, mostly. But the occasional painting." Miss Dalrymple always had a list of plants she wanted rendered, and Felicity believed her skills were improving. Miss Dalrymple seemed pleased with her work, yet Felicity was reticent to discuss it publicly.

When Louisa was also asked to dance, Felicity retreated to a corner of the room where she could see Lucy and remain out of Mr. Woodburn's view. Lucy danced with ease and was talking with her partner, signs that her earlier case of nerves had dissipated.

Felicity took advantage of the moment to search for Silas. He was still at the refreshment table with Edmund, and she decided to join them. Was it her imagination, or did Silas's face light up when he saw her?

Three young ladies walked by, skirts floating over the floor like silent bells. Evangeline Harris was one of them, and her eyes drifted to Edmund before her focus returned to her companions. They whispered to each other behind their fans, and Felicity wondered who the focus of their gossip was tonight.

Silas handed her a glass of lemonade. "Are you enjoying the evening?"

Felicity sipped the drink. It was too sweet for her liking, but at least with a drink in hand and in the company of two gentlemen, men like Mr. Woodburn might leave her alone. "Until this moment, I have found little to enjoy," Felicity said.

Silas tilted his head, raising an eyebrow. "But the night is full of possibilities."

"Maybe for you," she replied.

"Have you become jaded in your old age, Miss Wixom?" he asked, smiling at her.

"Why, yes, I believe I have. Have you become an insufferable optimist?"

He laughed. "Insufferable? I don't believe I have achieved that yet."

Edmund stepped between them. "I want to dance with Evangeline, but she is always surrounded by other ladies, and I fear they are ravening wolves eager to tear me apart if I approach."

Felicity glanced over at Evangeline, whose eyes were fixed on Edmund as she smiled at him and closed her fan.

"You have nothing to fear from them. They are much more likely to turn on each other than to turn on you," Felicity said. "Besides, Evangeline wants you to talk to her."

Edmund turned to her, perplexed. "How do you know that?"

"She closed her fan."

"Messages in fans, meanings in flowers, I'll never keep it all straight. Wish me luck." Edmund downed his drink and crossed the ballroom. Within moments, he and Evangeline were smiling and making their way to the dance floor.

"I've never seen Edmund take your advice so readily. What has changed?" Silas asked.

"He has failed in courtship before, and this time, I think he is serious about making it work. As you can see, when he takes my advice, things progress rather well. I do think even he won't be able to make a mess of things now. What about you? Are you in want of a wife?"

"I might be," he said.

"When you left for India, you were determined to remain carefree and unattached."

"I've had a change of heart," he said, tapping her on the nose as if she were a child.

Felicity playfully batted his hand. She wished they were not in a crowded ballroom with people milling all about. It was impossible to hold a conversation above the din, and she wanted to tell him about the rumors Louisa had heard. In private. "Let's go out on the terrace," she suggested.

He offered her his arm and escorted her away from the ballroom. The night air was cool and from the empty terrace, the music subsided into the background.

"You would be surprised what I am hearing about you in India," Felicity said, regarding him to see his reaction.

Silas grimaced. "I can only imagine."

"I hear you were nearly trampled by an elephant, could not eat the food and were very ill, married the daughter of one of the British generals, and that you were instrumental in thwarting an attempt to overthrow the East India Company in Bombay."

Silas tipped his head back and laughed. "I don't know where to begin with those stories."

"Perhaps the one where you got married?"

"I do not have a secret wife in India, Felicity," he said in all seriousness.

His denial of a relationship filled Felicity with relief. Rather than pause to consider her feelings, she moved on to the next rumor. "You arrived home so thin. Was the food not to your liking?"

"Oh, I liked it very much. But food was scarce when we fled Delhi, and I did not eat much on the ship home. I am, however, making up for that now. I brought some curry home with me. If you would like to try it, I'll see that your family is invited to dinner soon."

"I would like that. And I would have been most offended if you had married without telling me. But enough of these rumors. What was India like?"

Silas ran a hand over his face. "It was hot, Fliss. Hotter than anything I have ever experienced. We had to get up early to get any work done before the day became unbearable. I have never sweat so much before in my life."

Felicity remained quiet. Silas was finally willing to talk, and she was afraid to break the spell. Surely their mothers would not want him to be discussing details like sweating with her, but now that he had begun, she didn't want him to stop.

"We all required so many servants. Men to fan us, to hand us our clothing as we dressed, men to serve our food, men to shave us. It was unbelievable. In some ways, I was immensely spoiled."

"Why so many?"

"The Indian servants had their own rules about who can do which jobs. It was against their way of life for someone to do a job they considered beneath them. The man I worked for treated the natives very well, but that was not usually the case. I saw many people ill-treated, Felicity, and it disturbed me. In hindsight, I wonder if that contributed to the mutiny. In good conscience, I can no longer work for the East India Company."

"What will you do?" Felicity asked.

"Father's solicitor has agreed to train me."

"Would it be better to become a barrister?" Felicity asked.

"It would be more lucrative, but Fliss, I cannot stomach the thought. I would rather do paperwork than argue in court. Father thinks that is a failing of mine. He believes it will limit my ability to make a good match."

"Is that what you want? A good match?"

"When I was in India, I saw up close what a marriage could be like when a couple truly loved each other and their children. I do desire that for myself, but who would want me?"

Anyone would want you. The thought surprised her. Was he what she wanted? She doubted he would ever look at her as any-thing but Edmund's sister, despite the fact that he had tucked an orange blossom behind her ear. An orange blossom that she had pressed between the pages of a book.

"Since you lack wealth, you shall have to rely on your charm," Felicity said.

He snorted. "I fear that no woman will be impressed by my manners."

"You have to woo them, and you can learn to do that."

Silas leaned on the railing overlooking a garden. The new moon gave no light, and the place was shrouded in darkness. "You saw how inept I was discussing marigolds with you when I gave you that shawl. Mother was appalled. I shall make a mess of things."

"No, you won't," Felicity said. "If Edmund can do it, so can you. I shall help you. The way to a woman's heart is through flowers and letters, and both of those happen to be my area of expertise."

Silas met her gaze. "Would you really do that? Would you help me?"

"I would be happy to. When someone catches your eye, we shall put together the perfect bouquet to send her a message that will tickle her fancy. Now, tell me what plants you saw in India."

"You would have loved the gardens, Felicity. They were so colorful. I doubt the heat would have kept you away from them."

He described the gardens to her in such detail that she could envision the pathways lined with marigolds, hibiscus, and jasmine. She doubted that she would ever travel afar to see such beautiful sights, but Silas was making it come alive for her.

"Mr. Parker?"

Three young ladies came toward them. Lydia and Anne were Lucy's age, but Felicity did not recognize the other young woman. She edged back a step, leaving him to engage with them. It was obvious they were interested in him, and she wished to see if he returned that interest. Secretly, she hoped he did not.

Anne and the other young lady giggled and pushed Lydia forward. She stumbled, and her face reddened.

"What is your name, Miss?" Silas asked.

"Lydia," she said. "Was it true you were mauled by a tiger when you were in India and that is why you returned home? Is that where you got your scar?"

Silas paused before answering. "Yes, indeed. I lost two limbs in the attack, but thankfully, I had several to spare."

The two girls standing to either side burst into laughter, but the questioner appeared confused. "So, you are missing only one now? An arm? For you are standing on both legs," she said, her brow furrowed.

Silas appeared uncomfortable, despite his attempt at humor, and Felicity had had enough of this nonsense. "Mr. Parker, I believe you promised me this dance." She took his arm and glared at the girls. "Ladies, you should not believe everything you hear." They backed away, giggling.

Silas was quiet as they walked to the dance floor. When the music started, he said, "Thank you for rescuing me."

Felicity nodded toward the girls. "It was my opportunity to keep you in my debt."

To her relief, he laughed, and it made her stomach flutter. She and Silas had laughed together many times over the years and not once had she had this sensation. Why was she so aware of the warmth of his hand on her waist? Her pulse quickened as they danced.

"If I ask you something, will you tell me the truth?" His eyes were serious.

She missed a step and landed on his foot. She recovered and said, "I may not be the most accomplished dance partner, but I will always be honest with you."

He glanced around as if to make sure no one would overhear him. "I knew there would be some gossip, but until this moment, I brushed that aside. Are there other rumors about me?"

"What does your family say? Or Edmund?"

"Nothing. I think they are protecting me."

"I am not an expert in the gossip of Upper Pangford," Felicity said, not wanting to share with him everything she'd heard.

"Are people saying things that would prevent me from being a solicitor here?" Silas's hazel eyes were full of worry.

"I suppose the most damaging rumors I hear are about cowardice—that you fled at the first hint of an uprising."

He blanched, and the troubled look she'd seen when he came home returned to his eyes. She wondered what memories were haunting him.

"I would rather have been mauled by a tiger. At least that rumor preserved my dignity," he said.

"Hmm, that is a good rumor. The best one I've heard, though, is that you became a pagan and you have grown horns," she said.

He snorted. "Horns?"

"If you'll allow me...." She ran her gloved fingers through his hair, not caring who might be watching them. With one finger, she gently traced the scar above his eye.

He leaned toward her touch, and she had a sudden longing to feel the ridge of his scar and the softness of his hair without her gloves. His eyes scrutinized hers, and for a moment, she lost all sense of the music and the crowd, disappearing into him the way she got lost when she was painting. He had flecks of gold in his hazel eyes, something she had never noticed before. His whiskers shadowed his face, inviting her to run her fingers along his jaw.

She cleared her throat. "No horns, which is rather disappointing."

He didn't respond, and she worried she might have offended him. "I should not have told you the rumors. I'm sorry," she said.

His expression changed and he smiled. "Let them think what they wish to think. You know gossip is as fleeting as winter sunshine, and I believe if I ignore it, people will soon find someone else to talk about."

"I hope you are right." The music stopped, and she curtseyed. "Thank you for the dance."

They left the dance floor, and when they parted, she gathered her skirts and climbed the stairs to the landing, seeking escape from rumors, and silly young ladies, and new thoughts and feelings about Silas that she was not sure she wanted to entertain.

Silas stated he was interested in marriage and a family. She wondered if he would ever consider her, for she did not like to think about a future without him in it. But surely, if he were interested in her, he would have said something. And he had not, despite many opportunities to do so. If he married, the only way she could think of to preserve their friendship was to introduce him to someone who was her friend. Louisa would never do, as she needed to marry a man with a fortune.

Felicity saw the ladies in the ballroom with new eyes. Who would be a good match for Silas and also tolerate their continued friendship? She came up with one possibility: Beatrice Turner.

Chapter Ten

September 18, 1857

Upper Pangford, England

Silas watched her go and debated whether or not he should join her. Edmund was talking to Evangeline in the corner, and he didn't know who else to converse with. When Felicity had run her hand through his hair, he feared the pounding of his heart would make it leap right out of his chest. His feelings for her had grown while he was away, and now he needed to know if things had changed for her, too. Determined to find out, he followed Felicity up the stairs.

Silas joined her at the railing, and they gazed down at the ballroom. He remembered standing beside her on an evening quite like this one when they were children. He wondered if she remembered how they'd made up stories about the guests in all their finery.

"That gentleman has traveled from abroad just to be here tonight. He has been receiving messages from a secret admirer and hopes to discover her identity during the ball," he said, resting his arm on the railing and letting it brush up against hers.

She raised an eyebrow at him. "And just how do you know that?"

Disappointed that she did not remember their game, he turned his gaze back to the guests. "That lady despises her nephew and hopes to make a good match for him so that she may hand him off, with his tiresome antics, to some poor, un-suspecting bride."

To his great pleasure, Felicity snorted out a laugh.

"Oh!" she said. "And the nephew is equally eager to be away from his aunt. He has already decided to lower his standards this evening. If a woman under the age of forty pays him any attention at all, he shall consider proposing on the spot."

Silas chuckled. "You do remember."

She grinned at him. "It took me a moment, but I do recall the evening. Why was it just the two of us here? Where was Edmund? Mother never left me alone."

"I believe he'd taken ill that day with a cold."

Felicity had a vague memory of slipping into the sick room to tell Edmund about the guests, but he'd been tossing in a feverish sleep. By the time he'd recovered, the details of the ball were already slipping from her mind, not that he would have been particularly interested anyway.

"I am impressed that you remember so much," Felicity said, patting his arm.

Encouraged by her touch, he said, "You were often the bright spot in otherwise tedious situations."

"As were you," she replied.

She was so near, and for the moment, they were alone. He gathered his courage. Maybe now he should tell her what her letter meant to him that night on the road to Karnal.

She interrupted his thoughts. "Have you met the Turners? Miss Beatrice Turner is very charming, and I understand that she has her own fortune and does not need to marry for money. She is over there with her parents, in the lavender gown. I do believe you should make her acquaintance."

Silas had not expected the conversation to go in this direction. Maybe Felicity was letting him know she had no interest in pursuing anything with him.

"I shall go talk to them and when you join us, I shall introduce you. Wait here," Felicity said.

"For how long?" he asked.

She glared at him. "If you cannot figure out the timing, Mr. Parker, then you are not deserving of a woman like Miss Turner."

He forced a smile to disguise his disappointment over her indifference to him. "It's so easy to get a rise from you. I'll see you shortly."

With a huff, she whirled and flounced away. He watched her go, aware of the way her emotions shifted like the colors of a sunrise. He never grew tired of trying to coax a smile from her.

Felicity reached the Turners and engaged them in conversation. Her face was animated as she talked, and he found it captivating. She glanced once toward the balcony, and he took that as his cue, making his way down the grand staircase to the ballroom.

When he approached her, she gave him a dazzling smile. "Mr. Turner, Mrs. Turner, Miss Turner, it is with great pleasure that I introduce you to Mr. Silas Parker."

Silas bowed in greeting.

Mr. Turner frowned. "Silas Parker? Are you the son of Mr. George Parker?"

"Yes, I am," Silas said, without hesitation. His family had an impeccable reputation, and he was never ashamed of being associated with them.

"Which son are you?" Mr. Turner asked. "I am only aware of three."

Silas paused. This was an unfortunate turn of events. Being a fourth son was not a selling point in the marriage mart, and he was not sure he could turn it to his advantage.

"Mr. Parker has only recently returned from India," Felicity said, stepping in and breaking the tension.

She was rescuing him once again, as she had so many times before. He gave her a grateful look.

"India?" Miss Turner said. "How fascinating. I would like to hear more about it."

She lowered her chin and gazed up at him through her long, beautiful eyelashes. Felicity had educated him about the wiles young ladies used to garner attention from men, and Miss Turner apparently had great skill. Her startling green eyes only added to her appeal.

Felicity excused herself, leaving him with the Turners. The family was quite agreeable as they talked about India and his clerkship there. He did not tell them that he was now a former East India Company clerk and that he was seeking new employment. No, it was far better for him to win them over before letting them know of his financial situation.

"Miss Turner, may I have this dance?" he asked.

Beatrice accepted and placed her hand on his arm, allowing him to lead her to the dance floor. She was shorter than Felicity with delicate features.

"Tell me more about India," Miss Turner said. "It sounds so exotic."

Silas spoke in generalities. "India is vast. And hot. At least the areas where I was working."

"And how long have you known Felicity?"

"Her brother, Edmund, and I are good friends. I have known her since her years of climbing trees and skipping stones on the River Pang. She often had skinned knees."

Beatrice laughed. "Somehow, I don't have trouble picturing her doing any of those things. It is a wonder that she does not yet have a suitor. She has been so kind since I moved here and perhaps you can help me remedy that situation. Do you know of any eligible men?"

Silas did not answer immediately. If he wasn't good enough for Felicity, he should at least attempt to find someone who was. "Perhaps if you had a brother, Miss Turner."

"We are a household of daughters, I'm afraid. Still, I shall keep my eyes open."

Silas finished the set with Miss Turner and was not able to find either Edmund or Felicity again. At long last, the ball ended, and Silas joined his parents for the carriage ride home.

The evening had not been a complete failure. He was unsure what to make of Felicity. One moment, she was creating an easy intimacy between them that he desired, and the next moment, she was introducing him to someone else and offering her advice. Maybe he did not know her as well as he thought. Or maybe, when it came to the two of them, she was as uncertain about their future as he was.

Chapter Eleven

September 22, 1857

Upper Pangford, England

Silas adjusted his waistcoat and smoothed his cravat before entering Mr. Crawford's office. The room held one large desk with two chairs in front of it, and a smaller desk tucked in a corner. Shelves filled with legal books filled the wall behind the large desk.

Father had secured him this position to train as a solicitor, and he was eager to get started in this new life. Mr. Crawford had either not heard all the rumors about him or did not give the gossip much thought. Either way, Silas was determined to take advantage of the opportunity.

Mr. Crawford was a stout, balding man. He welcomed Silas and gestured for him to take a seat opposite the desk. "It has been a while since I trained someone," the man said. "It is my custom to start by going over papers and having you perform simple tasks at first, but I have an appointment this morning, and I think it would be beneficial for you to accompany me.

"Very well." Silas followed Mr. Crawford to a waiting carriage.

"I have more work than I can manage right now, and I am hoping you will be a quick study with your clerical experience," Mr. Crawford said. "This morning, we shall be reviewing some paperwork related to the estate and also discussing a potential marriage settlement."

"Marriage settlement?" Silas asked.

"Yes. Our client wishes to draw one up for his eldest daughter. He wants to make sure an allowance will be available to her when she marries and that all of her wealth will not go to her husband. I don't know if any property is involved in the desired contract, but we shall see."

This meeting would be a good opportunity for Silas to familiarize himself with marriage contracts and inheritance law, and he was eager to begin. The carriage turned down a lane he knew well, and a knot formed in his stomach as they approached Ashwick Manor.

"We are meeting with Mr. Wixom?" he asked. Why had Felicity not told him of an impending marriage? He shrank back against the carriage seat, his cravat tight against his throat.

"Yes. Are you familiar with the family?"

"We are of long acquaintance," he said.

"Good, then they will not object to you being here today. I must remind you that our conversations are confidential, and you are here simply to observe."

"Yes, sir," Silas said. His palms were damp, and he rubbed them on his trousers. He was more nervous meeting with Mr. Wixom than he would be with a stranger.

The carriage stopped and they got out and climbed the steps to the door. The butler ushered them into the library where Mr. Wixom sat behind his desk. Edmund occupied a chair near his father, and his eyes widened when he saw Silas.

"Mr. Wixom, might I introduce my new junior solicitor, Silas Parker."

"Welcome, Silas. Your father must be glad to see you put your time to good use," Mr. Wixom said.

Silas nodded, and took a seat, determined to keep quiet and learn.

Mr. Crawford laid some documents on the desk. "Here is the updated paperwork you requested. It details what Mr. Edmund will inherit from the estate, and, as we also discussed, I have listed some of my recommendations for a marriage settlement for Miss Wixom."

Edmund rose from his chair and peered over his father's shoulder. "Are you planning to make a similar arrangement for Lucy?"

Mr. Wixom nodded. "When the time comes."

Silas longed to ask when Felicity was to be married, and to whom, but in keeping with Mr. Crawford's wishes, he remained silent.

Edmund continued to read over the papers. "That is a significant sum. I believe Felicity will find it most generous."

Mr. Wixom grunted. "Your sister deserves to be taken care of. But it is a substantial amount, and it mustn't become public knowledge. I do not wish to have to fend off prospective suitors that only hope to have a claim on her money. It would be far better for her to choose someone of similar means who did not need her money for their own support."

Did Mr. Wixom's mention of prospective suitors mean Fliss was not yet promised to someone? Hope surged through him. But then again, Mr. Wixom did have concerns about men only being interested in her for her money. Even if he were to muster the courage to court her, now that he was aware of her allowance, he feared her father would be suspicious of his motives. He should have talked to her long ago, and now he may have missed his chance.

The gentlemen discussed some changes to the documents and Mr. Crawford handed the papers to Silas. "If we might use your pen, Mr. Wixom, I'll have my assistant make notes of what we've discussed."

Silas took the pen and bent to his task, not meeting Edmund's eyes. He feared his own expression would give away his growing feelings for Felicity. Feelings he must now deny.

Mr. Crawford had Silas take the documents when they were finished. "We shall hold them in the office until you have need of them. Now, here are the updates for your estate." Mr. Wixom, Edmund, and Mr. Crawford soon became engrossed in the nuances of the paperwork. Silas tried to pay attention, but Felicity filled his thoughts.

After the Harvest Ball, he'd intended to give her the letter he wrote to her from Karnal. He had carried it with him throughout his long journey home and he'd kept it safe, waiting for the right moment to give it to her. But now, he didn't think that moment would ever come. He was grateful that he had never mentioned his intentions to Edmund, or to Felicity herself. She deserved the best the world could offer her. As for himself, he would have to find someone else.

When their business was finished, Silas collected the papers and stacked them neatly. He bowed to Mr. Wixom and accompanied his employer outside to the graveled drive.

Edmund followed Silas. "So, this is your new venture?"

"Yes, if all goes well, I shall be a fully qualified solicitor soon," Silas said. It would be a solid career, and he would not apologize for it.

"And this is what you want?" Edmund asked.

Silas did not have to look at Mr. Crawford to know that the man was listening to whatever he said. Silas was very lucky to find a local solicitor willing to train him, and he did not want to lose the position. "Yes, Mr. Crawford has an excellent reputation, and I am quite fortunate he has given me this opportunity."

Edmund eyed him closely, then shrugged. "I like the idea of having you as my solicitor in the future. Someone I can trust. Good luck to you."

Silas tipped his hat. He was anxious to leave before he ran into Felicity. He couldn't imagine Felicity married to someone else. He had only begun to imagine courting her himself, and now he would lose her to another. No man would let his wife maintain a friendship with another man.

He couldn't deny the marriage settlement in the sheaf of papers in his hands. He knew what he must do. The letter he'd written to Felicity in India was tucked away safely in his room at home where it would stay. Perhaps he should go home and burn it. Destroy any evidence that his feelings toward her had changed. It would never do for her to find out something like that now, something that neither of them could act on. He'd promised Lucy that he would never hurt her, and he would keep that promise no matter the personal cost.

He waited impatiently for the carriage to be brought around. Mr. Crawford stood stiffly beside him, gazing up at the gray sky.

"Silas!" Felicity strode across the drive. A servant followed her, carrying an easel and paint box. Tendrils of hair escaped the knot at the back of her head and curled around her face. Her cheeks were rosy from the cool autumn air. She held a painting in her hands, and her happiness was unmistakable. She stopped when she saw them.

"Mr. Crawford, Mr. Parker, what business brings you here this morning?"

"We were discussing estate matters with your father," Mr. Crawford said.

Silas gestured at the canvas in her hands. "What are you painting?"

She turned the canvas toward him. "I wanted to paint the ash tree while the leaves are gold."

Her painting showed the tree, resplendent with warm yellow leaves against a cloudy, gray sky. "Your paintings astound me," he said.

"Thank you. It isn't finished yet, but I am happy with the progress. How are you enjoying your work with Mr. Craw-ford?"

"I am learning things I did not anticipate," he said.

"Oh?"

The carriage arrived and Mr. Crawford got inside. Silas took a deep breath. "Yes. Am I to congratulate you on your upcoming marriage?"

"Why would you ask that?" Her brow wrinkled in confusion.

"I thought maybe you had neglected to tell me your good news." He straightened the papers in his hand, bracing himself for her reply.

"And would it be good news?" She put a hand on her hip and held his gaze.

"Yes, I mean, no. Not for me. I would regret losing our friendship. But I would be happy for you, if a marriage is what you want." He wondered if saying it out loud would make it true. But if Felicity were planning to get married, he might be able to be happy for her, but he would have deep regrets for himself. The realization gave him pause.

"There is no wedding, Silas. I don't know what gave you that idea, but I must disavow you of it."

The tightness in his chest loosened and he could breathe easily once again. "I'm sorry if I got the wrong idea. Your father had Mr. Crawford prepare papers for your marriage settlement and I thought...."

"Are you coming, Mr. Parker?" Mr. Crawford poked his head out of the carriage.

"Right away," Silas called. He turned back to Felicity. "I was supposed to keep that meeting confidential. I'm sorry I mentioned it." But, if he was honest with himself, he was not sorry that Felicity was not getting married.

"I will not let on that I know, but it will be interesting to see if I can get Edmund to confess the details."

"Edmund is no match for you," Silas said with a grin.

"Mr. Parker, I insist that you come," Mr. Crawford said, leaning out of the carriage once more.

Felicity called to the man, "Mr. Crawford, might I trouble you to wait a few more minutes? I have something to discuss with Mr. Parker."

Mr. Crawford grunted in response, but he sat back inside the carriage.

Felicity handed the painting to a footman and asked him to take it to the house. She turned back to Silas. "Have you called on Miss Turner?"

"I called on her the day after the ball and it went well," Silas said. "But that is not why you asked Mr. Crawford to wait."

"I need a favor, and I thought I would ask you since you are my solicitor now."

"Solicitor in training, and your father is Mr. Crawford's client," he said.

She moved close to him. "If I needed to send a letter to London without my family's knowledge, would you post it for me?"

He tipped her chin up, searching her face. "You're not in any trouble, are you?"

"No, not at all. But if I send this letter, I will need to have any replies come through you."

He wavered. As her friend, he wanted to help her, but he also had a responsibility to his employer and to her father. "If your father finds out, will he be upset with me? With Mr. Craw-ford?"

She laid a hand on his arm. "I'm sorry I asked. I do not want to put your job at risk."

Her blue eyes held his gaze, steady and unflinching. Did she understand that he could not refuse her?

"Get the letter to me, and I will take care of it," he said.

"Are you sure?"

"Yes. You know I would do anything for you, Fliss."

"Thank you, Silas."

He climbed aboard the carriage, and as they pulled away, he gazed after her. Her steps were light, and she skipped a step as she made her way to the house. He sat back against the carriage seat with a sigh, wondering what he had just agreed to. He would wait to find out before he asked her if he could court her. He did not wish to reveal his growing feelings for her if there was little chance she would return them. And whatever it was she wanted, he would not stand in her way.

Chapter Twelve

September 28, 1857

Upper Pangford, England

Miss Dalrymple stopped by to see Felicity's latest work. Felicity led her up to the morning room and pulled her most recent drawings out of her writing desk. Miss Dalrymple did not speak as she examined them, and Felicity waited with nervous anticipation for her reaction.

"These are splendid, Miss Wixom. I believe you have made great improvement. I am fortunate to have found you before you are in greater demand."

"What do you mean?" Felicity asked.

"Once we show your drawings and paintings combined with my research, other scientists will want you to work for them. You could do anything you want, Miss Wixom."

"What if I wish to go to art school?"

Miss Dalrymple eyed her thoughtfully. "This work would make you a good candidate. But why do you wish to go? Are you interested in doing more than botanical work?"

"Yes," Felicity said eagerly. "I want to learn more about color and landscapes and perspective and...." She shook her head. "But my family would never support me in it."

Miss Dalrymple glanced at the drawings once again. "It would be a shame to waste your talent, Miss Wixom. I will not lie to you. Pursuing your dream may cost you in our society. I am a good example of that. I fight every day to be taken seriously as a scientist, and I do not have the blessing of a companion and children in my life."

"Do you have any regrets?" Felicity asked.

Miss Dalrymple smiled. "Not a one. My work fulfills me. But you must consider carefully what it is you really want. If art school is your dream, you must find a way, even if it means disappointing people you love."

"Did you lose your family over your dreams?"

"What worked for me may not work for you. I did lose my family for a time, but they are no longer ashamed of me. I dare say my sister is even quite proud of what I do. My advice to you, my dear, is that if you get a chance, take it."

Mrs. Wixom entered the room to do her morning correspondence. She stopped in surprise to see Miss Dalrymple there.

"I was just leaving," Miss Dalrymple said. "Your daughter's artwork has far exceeded my expectations. You must be very proud of her. Good day."

Mrs. Wixom seemed very surprised and barely managed a response. When Miss Dalrymple left, she turned to her daughter. "What was that all about?"

"She was pleased with my drawings," Felicity said.

Mrs. Wixom said nothing more as she sat at her desk and began reading through her morning mail.

Felicity's pulse pounded. She had nearly talked herself out of applying to art school, but if she didn't apply, she knew in her heart she would always regret not knowing what she could have done. Her hands trembled as she got out a fresh piece of paper and began to compose a letter to the Female Academy of Art.

If she did not get accepted, there was no need to upset her family. If she did get accepted, she would cross that bridge when she came to it. But even as she wrote, she wondered what Silas would think. She had missed him so much when he was away, did she want to leave him and go to school in London now that they were finally reunited?

Still, if he ended up marrying someone, it would be better for her heart to be at a distance from him.

She sealed the letter and addressed it quickly, blotting the ink dry. Now she only had to get it to Silas and he would send it for her. Whether her venture succeeded or failed, she would at least know that she had tried. Miss Dalrymple was right. She had to take the chance while she could.

Mother glanced up from her correspondence. "Felicity, there is a musicale tonight at the James's house. Shall I respond for both of us? Mr. Woodburn will be in attendance."

Felicity groaned. "Mr. Woodburn's oldest child is Lucy's age, Mother. I have no desire to spend an evening with the man."

"Now, dear, he would be a suitable match for you despite his age. You would want for nothing in his household."

Want for nothing except her freedom. "I don't believe I shall ever love him, Mother, and I wish to marry for love or not at all."

"Felicity, I am dismayed you have fallen for such modern notions. Mr. Woodburn would ...."

Edmund burst into the room, and Felicity was grateful for the interruption. She had no desire to continue discussing Mr. Woodburn.

"Good morning, Mother! Father wants me to go to London on an errand for him, and I'd like to take Felicity with me. We'll stay at the house for two nights. After my business tomorrow, I'll take her to Kew Gardens."

Felicity perked up at the mention. She loved Palm House in the Gardens and was eager to see its extensive tropical plant collection again. While they were there, they could also explore the ferneries and the Orchideous House.

"Mother, are you still planning to have Ashwick Manor be part of the fall garden tour?" Felicity asked.

Mother nodded. "Yes. It is coming up quite soon."

"If I go with Edmund, I'll be able to get more ideas for plants for the conservatory. May I go?"

To her delight, Mother agreed.

"I will be packed and ready within the hour," Felicity told Edmund. She hurried to her room and tucked the letter to the art school in her handbag. If she could slip away in London to send it herself, she needn't trouble Silas and risk anyone being upset at his involvement.

Her maid helped her change into a dress suitable for traveling and packed dresses to wear at Kew Gardens and on the journey home. She gathered a night dress, underthings, and a shawl. "I hear the London house is cold, Miss. You might want it."

Felicity fingered the heavy gray material. Writing the letter to the art school and heading to London made her feel bold. Daring. She handed the shawl back to the maid. "Please put this one away and bring me the shawl from Mr. Parker."

The maid nodded and hurried to fetch it. Felicity packed the shawl carefully inside her small trunk, put on her hat, and went to meet Edmund. He was waiting for her in front of the house beside the carriage.

To her surprise, when she entered the carriage, Silas was already there.

"What are you doing here?" she said, smiling at him.

"I needed to go to London on business, and Edmund suggested I ride with both of you."

"Splendid," she said. This day kept getting better and better.

Edmund climbed in and sat beside his friend.

"Are you surprised?" Edmund asked.

"Yes," she said. "Silas, will you be staying with us?"

Silas shook his head. "No. I am staying at an inn tonight. To-morrow, I will conduct my business on behalf of Mr. Crawford and then take a coach back to Upper Pangford."

Felicity settled back in her seat, content to be with Edmund and Silas once again. They were soon off. The journey would take most of the day, but the horses were fresh, and they would only need to make a few stops to rest them.

"Speaking of Mr. Crawford, what were you and Father meeting with him about, Edmund?"

"My inheritance, and your marriage settlement," Edmund said. She was surprised that getting the information from him had taken no effort at all.

"Is this for a marriage I don't yet know about?"

"No," Edmund said. "Father wishes you to be happily wed, and he is making provisions so that if that occurs, you will also be taken care of financially, that's all. I don't believe he has anyone in mind for you."

"I hope you are right," she said, thinking of her earlier conversation with Mother about Mr. Woodburn.

"Now that we are together once again, there must be some mischief we can find," Edmund said.

"We are too old for mischief, Edmund," Silas said.

"Speak for yourself. I have something planned, but you must send word to Mr. Crawford that you need to stay in London an extra day. Then you can accompany us to Kew Gardens."

Felicity saw Silas's hesitation. "You must come with us. It will be like old times."

"I suppose I could," he said.

"It's settled, then." Edmund reached for the basket resting on the seat beside Felicity. He pulled out pastries and handed them each one. "I brought these to celebrate the three musketeers being reunited. To us!"

Silas shook his head but tapped his pastry against Edmund's. "I have never made a toast with a treat before."

Felicity grinned. "To the three musketeers. May we never be disbanded."

They each bit into the flaky layers, savoring the jam-filled centers.

Edmund's knee jounced up and down, and he could not sit still.

"What are you not telling us?" Felicity asked.

"You will both know soon enough," Edmund said with a grin.

Felicity sighed. She hoped his surprise would be a pleasant one.

When they stopped to rest and water the horses, Edmund left the carriage to stretch his legs. Felicity pulled the letter out of her handbag and gave it to Silas.

"This is what I need you to post. When you are about your business tomorrow, will you send it for me?"

He glanced at it before tucking it into the pocket of his waist-coat. "I'll see to it. Art school," he mused. "Will you be drawing the human figure if you are accepted?"

"Hardly. The school for ladies focuses more on design than the human figure, but I believe I will still be able to improve my skills. You won't tell Edmund, will you?" she asked as her brother approached the carriage.

Silas shook his head. "Your secret is safe with me."

Edmund stuck his head in the carriage. "Felicity, you move over by Silas. I wish to trade places for the next part of the journey."

She rolled her eyes. "You only want to be near the food and I have to maneuver a hoop skirt. I'm not moving."

He laughed. "I can't have you eating it all. Go on. Move."

Silas got up and lifted the basket, setting it on the spot he vacated. "I'll sit by Felicity. There is no need for her to move just for you."

"You always take her side," Edmund said, flopping onto the carriage seat.

"He knows what's good for him," Felicity said.

Edmund leaned forward, studying them.

"What are you doing?" Felicity asked.

"Trying to picture your offspring."

Silas squirmed in the seat, but Felicity was quick to respond. "Think of the most adorable child you have ever seen. That is what my children will look like. Yours, however, had best take after Evangeline."

Chapter Thirteen

September 29, 1857

Kew Gardens, London

Felicity entered Palm House and inhaled the familiar warm air. Edmund's business had not taken long, and they had arrived at Kew Gardens in the early afternoon. She heard voices as more people entered the building. To her delight, Silas was there, too, his brown hair a bit disheveled.

As he greeted her, she caught sight of Evangeline Harris and Beatrice Turner coming inside. They waved to her and headed in her direction.

Felicity made no effort to mask her disappointment as she confronted Edmund. "You said it would be the three muske-teers on an adventure today. You didn't warn me I am here to be a chaperone for your romantic escapades. You have Silas. And Beatrice. Why did you need me?"

Now rather than an enjoyable afternoon with Edmund and Silas, she would be the person left out while they paired up with their respective ladies. It was unfair of Edmund. And frustrating.

Edmund shrugged. "You have your plants. I have Evangeline, and Silas has Miss Turner. I thought you would enjoy the Gardens."

Felicity glared at him, but he seemed not to notice as he went to Evangeline.

"I took care of your business this morning," Silas said, quietly, so no one else heard.

"Thank you." At least her letter was off to the art school. Now she must wait for a response.

Beatrice hurried forward and gripped Felicity's hands. "It's lovely to see you! I'm so happy you are on this outing with us today."

"The pleasure is all mine," Felicity said, even though she didn't mean it. It was obvious that Beatrice and Evangeline were here at Edmund's invitation, and that her brother hadn't wanted her to know until this moment.

Beatrice turned to Silas. "And Mr. Parker, it is good to see you, also." She glanced demurely at him from beneath her long eyelashes while Silas stammered a response. It wasn't like Silas to be at a loss for words. Did he care for Miss Turner after such a short acquaintance?

Felicity hid her disappointment that their group had expanded to five. Edmund and Evangeline were already heading off together, arm in arm, heads tilted together in conversation. She suspected that Silas and Beatrice would soon follow. Rather than being awkwardly left alone, she took charge of the situation. It was best to be practical, and Beatrice would be a great catch for Silas. "Mr. Parker, perhaps you would accompany Miss Turner today as I will be spending so much time examining plants that you will find I am not good company," she said.

Beatrice smiled at Felicity and took Silas's arm. Silas raised an eyebrow as if asking if she was certain he should go with Miss Turner. Trust Silas to be concerned about her feelings.

"You two go ahead," Felicity assured him. "I will be fine by myself." But as he walked away from her with Beatrice, she longed to be with someone. It was all well and good to talk about remaining a spinster, but seeing Edmund and Silas with other partners caused her to wonder if she would be happy alone.

The autumn sun streamed through the glass walls. and Felicity spun slowly in a circle, trying to decide where to start. She could stay here for days, sketching and painting. She decided to head in the opposite direction of the two couples. That way, she would not have to listen to what might be an enthusiastic conversation between Beatrice and Silas, or an overly sentimental conversation between Edmund and Evangeline.

She paused by an interesting plant with dark purple and red foliage. It was labeled as a ti plant from Malaya. Such a plant would be beautiful in her conservatory. She wondered how difficult it would be to get one. She surveyed it from different angles, trying to memorize the shape of the leaves and the nuances of the color so that she could paint it when she arrived home. She made a mental note to check with the flower shop man to see if he knew where she might purchase one.

Felicity climbed to the upper walkway and stopped by green, palm-like leaves of the oldest plant in the house. It was a cycad, she recalled, although taxonomy was not her strong suit. Miss Dalrymple told her the plant had come to England in 1775. Now it was over seven feet tall, but from the height of the walkway, she could view the tops of its leafy branches.

She leaned on the railing and gazed over the entire Palm House. Edmund and Evangeline had eyes only for each other. She suspected if she asked Edmund what plants he had admired when they got back to the London house that evening, he would not be able to name a single one. She wouldn't be surprised at all if Edmund asked Evangeline for her hand in marriage soon.

Beatrice and Silas emerged from behind some sort of palm. Silas trailed after Beatrice who stopped occasionally to point out something to him. They didn't seem to have much to say to each other, and Silas's posture was stiff. Oh dear, this would not do at all. Felicity hurried down from the walkway and headed toward them, wondering what she could do to start a comfortable conversation between them.

"There she is," Beatrice said as Felicity approached. "Have you gotten your fill of plants, yet? Mr. Parker and I have exhausted our botanical knowledge and I, for one, am willing to leave at any time."

"I'm afraid I've only begun here, but it is such a pleasant day that maybe you and Mr. Parker would enjoy a walk outside. It would enable you to see more of the Gardens." She did not add that it would also be a chance for them to get to know one another better. "Mr. Parker might be interested in where you lived before your move to Upper Pangford." She gave Silas a meaningful glance.

"I would like that very much," Silas said to Beatrice. He offered her his arm and the two exited Palm House, chatting amiably about horses and archery.

Felicity focused on the plants. Every plant was exotic in its own way, and she longed to return with a sketchbook. Thanks to the encouragement of Miss Dalrymple, her collection of paintings and drawings had grown considerably. She glanced at Edmund, who was engrossed in whatever Evangeline was saying.

She left Palm House and followed a trail past a meadow where purple asters bloomed. She continued on to the Ferneries, keeping an eye out for Silas. She found herself watching for him whenever she knew he was in the area, always hoping for a bit of conversation or the brush of his arm against hers. She found herself comparing every man she met to him, and they always came up lacking. Now she wished she were in Beatrice's place, that she was the one holding Silas's arm.

If she were walking with him now, she'd show him the flowers she admired. It was too bad the rhododendrons bloomed in the spring, for she heard they were quite lovely. Had Silas seen them in India? She made a mental note to ask him. Time slipped by, and before she knew it, she was being summoned by Edmund.

"Have you seen Beatrice? Evangeline is waiting for her by their carriage, and ours will be here for us soon," he said.

"I lost track of them when they left Palm House," she said.

She and Edmund went in opposite directions to look for them, agreeing to meet near the entrance to the Gardens.

Felicity hurried down a path, searching. She spotted Silas back near Palm House where they had started and, to her relief, Beatrice was with him. "Edmund says the carriages are waiting," she said.

"When will you be back in Upper Pangford?" Beatrice asked Silas.

"I shall return with the Wixoms tomorrow," Silas said.

"You must come to call when you are back," Beatrice said.

Silas tipped his hat. "I would like that very much."

Felicity knew she should be pleased that their courtship was off to a good start, but if she were honest with herself, she was afraid of losing Silas and their friendship.

The group strolled to the waiting carriages. "I wish you could ride with me and Beatrice," Evangeline said to Edmund.

He took her hand in his. "I promised Mother I would keep an eye on Felicity."

Felicity huffed. She did not need Edmund to mind her.

Evangeline stuck out her lower lip in a childish pout. Edmund leaned toward her, his eyes focused on her mouth.

Evangeline touched his cheek. "You said Silas is like a brother to you. No one would think twice if he escorted Felicity back to your London house. You could dine with me and Beatrice at my parents' home."

Edmund clasped Evangeline's gloved hand. "You are persuasive, but I am afraid I must ride with Silas and Felicity. I shall count the minutes until we are together again." He kissed the back of her hand.

The footman opened the door and Felicity climbed inside, eager to be away from the courting couples. First Silas and then Edmund handed the ladies into their waiting carriage, and at long last, they joined her for the ride into London. Edmund got into the carriage first and sat next to her. Silas sat across from Edmund.

"Edmund, it appears you and Evangeline got everything you desired from this visit. What about you, Silas? Did you and Beatrice find things to talk about?" Felicity asked.

"I enjoyed spending time with Miss Turner," Silas said. "But it was very different than an afternoon with you and Edmund."

Felicity did not press him further. If he preferred Beatrice's company to hers, she did not want to know. As the carriage started forward, gray clouds rolled across the sky, blocking out the sun. Felicity was grateful to be inside the carriage when the rain started. At first it was a gentle patter, but as they drove into London, the rain came down in sheets.

Silas nudged her arm. "What was your favorite thing today?"

"The old cycad was beautiful, but I loved the ti plants. I must see if I can get some for the conservatory."

"If you do, you'll have to show them to me. Have you added many plants in the past few weeks?" he asked.

Before Felicity could respond, a loud cracking sound filled the air followed by the screech of iron and wood on the cobblestone road. The carriage tilted. Silas took her hand and squeezed it quite hard.

"What the devil?" Edmund asked. He struggled to open the carriage door and stepped outside.

Felicity tried to free her hand, but Silas's pale face stopped her. "Are you all right?" she asked.

He blinked and released her. "I'm fine. That sound." He swallowed hard. "It reminded me of something I have tried hard to forget."

Edmund poked his head inside the carriage, dripping wet. "An axle broke, but we are not far from the house. I believe we can walk from here."

Felicity followed him out into the rain, Silas close behind her. "I shall go to the inn," he said.

"Nonsense," Edmund replied. "I will send someone for your things, and you can stay with us. I'll arrange for another carriage in the morning, and we'll all return to Upper Pangford together."

Edmund spoke to the driver who was already unhitching the horses. Felicity trudged through the rain, her shoes and skirt soon soaked. Edmund said they were close to the London house, but it was quite clear to her that his idea of close was far different from her own. She longed for an umbrella as water dripped from the edge of her bonnet. At least the staff was expecting them, and there would be a hot dinner and dry clothes ahead.

The three of them walked together, Felicity aware of Silas hovering near her, as if he took comfort from her presence. She wondered what had upset him, and wished she dared to take his hand, to let him know everything was all right. But for now, she took comfort from the fact that the three musketeers were reunited, if only for one night.

Chapter Fourteen

September 29-30, 1857

The Wixom house, London

The candle flickered as Silas crept down the hallway. After tossing and turning for what seemed like hours, he'd given up on sleep. He paused outside Felicity's door and listened. All was quiet. He made his way downstairs and parted the heavy draperies in the drawing room. The rain had stopped and reflections from the gas lamps illuminated the wet street. The drapes fell as he left the window and sat on a chair, wondering if it would be permissible to go to the kitchen to find something to eat. While dinner had been adequate, he was restless and eating something would, he hoped, soothe him.

It wasn't the first time Silas had been a guest in the Wixom's London home. He and Felicity had slept under the same roof on multiple occasions over the years when Silas and Edmund were in school.

But his favorite memories of Edmund and Felicity were from their time together in Upper Pangford. Once when he was fifteen and Felicity was eleven, he and Edmund had planned a day of fishing. Felicity had slipped out of the house and trailed after them. While they attempted to fish, Felicity tossed rocks into the river. The larger the splash, the more annoyed Edmund had become, and the more annoyed he was, the larger the rocks she tossed. When she had refused to stop despite Edmund's best efforts, Silas gave up on fishing and taught her to skip rocks instead. Edmund had lain on the riverbank, hat over his eyes, and had fallen asleep. Finally, Felicity had grown tired of the game, and Silas was able to catch a very small fish. They had used it for bait to catch crayfish that day. Edmund had wanted to take the crayfish home for dinner, but Felicity insisted on returning them to the river. She had balanced on a rock at the edge of the water, and while letting the creatures go, she stretched too far, lost her balance, and splashed into the water. Edmund had laughed while Silas grabbed her arm and helped her out. To punish Edmund for laughing, she'd thrown her arms around him, soaking him in a wet embrace.

How he had loved spending time with Edmund and Felicity growing up. The Wixom household was peaceful compared to the cramped quarters of his own home with three boisterous older brothers.

"Can't sleep?" Felicity's voice pulled him from his reverie.

"No," he shook his head, standing up from the chair. "I always find it difficult to sleep the first night in a strange place."

"We should leave you behind tomorrow when we go then, so that you can sleep well the second night," she said.

He chuckled at that as she came toward him, wearing the paisley shawl over her nightdress. Her hair hung over one shoulder in a braid. Strands escaped and curled around her cheeks and forehead. The flickering candlelight danced across her cheeks and made her eyes sparkle, and he longed to smooth the strands of hair away from her face.

"You're wearing the shawl," he said.

She fingered the soft fabric. "I am. An old friend gave it to me." She winked at him. "Are you hungry?"

"Are you?" he asked, not wanting to inconvenience her if she was not on her way to the kitchen.

"I am. Care to join me?"

He trailed after her, fully aware of her thin nightdress and bare feet. He leaned against a kitchen counter as she added coal to the stove and filled a kettle with water. She moved around the kitchen with practiced ease.

"You are quite handy," he said. "What other talents are you hiding from me?"

Felicity wrinkled her nose at him. "Mother insisted I learn how to manage a household. She, no doubt, is more disappointed by my continued spinsterhood than anyone. She always wanted me to fill her later years with the laughter of grandchildren, but I am afraid Edmund and Evangeline shall have that burden. And Lucy. She may marry before any of us."

"You are not very old," Silas said. "You have plenty of time if you want children. Do you?"

She shrugged as she rummaged through a cupboard, pulling out a bit of bread. "There is no point in focusing my desire on things I cannot have. I have endured several London seasons and not found any men interesting enough to make a lifetime commitment to them. I am tired of the whole charade." She paused. "Do you think I am wasting my time, Silas? Pursuing things I cannot have, like art school? Do you think I should be taking on a husband, even if he is twenty years older than me?"

His eyes widened in alarm. "Have you had such an offer?"

She peered past him as if she expected a servant or Edmund to be nearby, listening. "Mother and Father have suggested some available men in the neighborhood, men who are widowed and in want of a wife to finish raising their children. But I don't believe they really want a wife. They want a woman to fill the role of hostess and governess. I don't think I would mind doing those things in my own family, but I could not step into that role for someone else's convenience. I would have to love the gentleman, and I do not have feelings for Mr. Woodburn, no matter how much Mother would like me to."

While the tea steeped, Felicity buttered two slices of bread. She handed one to Silas. "I'm sorry I don't have more to offer. Do you want me to check the larder?"

He shook his head. "It's decadent to be able to walk into a room and find bread waiting."

"Decadent?"

"In India, when we escaped Delhi, we soon ran out of food. Sometimes the people in the villages we passed traded with us for something to eat. Once they even brought us milk for the children. But other times we were not so fortunate." His hand went to the scar on his face.

"I can't imagine what you went through. How do you manage to maintain a positive view of life?" she asked as she poured their tea.

This domestic side of Felicity was unfamiliar to him. Not at all like the girl who frightened fish by skipping stones at the river. It was appealing.

He ran a fingernail along a groove in the counter. "Before I left India, a friend told me I had the chance at a fresh start and that I get to choose what I do with it. Sometimes it is impossible to choose to see the sunny side of things, but on the days that I can, I do my best to follow that counsel." He sipped his tea, savoring the way the hot liquid warmed him inside. The silence between them was comfortable.

"Were you in a great deal of danger?" she asked.

He considered how much to tell her. He hoped if he did not talk about what happened, the entire experience would subside into the dark recesses of his mind. But so far, on nights like tonight, the memories were all too clear.

"Because my employer and his wife were so good to their servants, they helped us escape Delhi. We retreated to Flagstaff Tower, and from there, we made our way to Karnal. Except Mr. Talbot. He was not with us, and I don't know what happened to him."

"I heard people were killed at the Main..." she paused. "Main Gate?"

"The Main Guard. Yes, the soldiers there turned on the British people who were seeking safety. I was fortunate and did not see it happen." He did not tell her about the arrival of the cart of bodies at Flagstaff Tower.

"And your scar?" she asked softly, tracing it with her finger.

He caught her hand and held it, rubbing his thumb across her palm. "I caught a rock with my head."

He tried to make a joke of it, but the images of people shouting at him and hurling rocks while he tried to protect Mrs. Talbot and the children were no laughing matter.

"I cannot decide if it makes you look dashing or damaged." She squinted at him in the dark.

"I am definitely damaged," he said. "I saw things I cannot erase from my mind. People being attacked. People dying. Sometimes they haunt my sleep."

She laced her fingers through his and her touch steadied him as the torrent of memories spilled out. He could not stop the words. He did not want to.

"The native troops outnumbered the British, and when they turned on us, we didn't have a chance. I fled in a cart under the cover of dirty laundry. When we got out of the city, people threw rocks at us and shouted. I had to look through bodies to try to identify my employer. We were lucky to escape. So many people did not. We left Flagstaff Tower under the cover of night, and I walked to the point of exhaustion in the dark."

Her hand squeezed his.

"And there, as we camped, I read your letter, Fliss. The one with the forget-me-nots, and I didn't feel so alone. I prayed I would make it out alive and find my way home."

"I was so worried about you," she said. "I cannot imagine how it was for you, being in the middle of all of that."

The burden he'd been carrying was lifted as he shared it with her. Now, however, he worried that he'd told her too much. He tried to make light of the situation.

"It was terrifying," he said. "But perhaps not half so frightening as coming back to society in Upper Pangford."

She gave him a wry smile and released his hand.

"Are there no eligible men in the neighborhood close to your age?" he asked.

She shook her head. "You and Edmund are the only two who are here, although I expect neither of you will be available much longer. I think you and Beatrice might form an attachment."

Silas set his cup down on the saucer. "Miss Turner is intriguing, but sometimes it is difficult to know what to say to her. I imagine if I spend enough time with her, she will realize she can do far better."

"How can you say such things? Any woman would be lucky to have you, Silas." She offered him more tea.

He shook his head. "A fourth son who aspires to be a lowly solicitor is not any woman's dream, and I doubt I fit her parents' vision for their daughter." He almost added that he didn't think he was good enough for the Wixoms daughter either but stopped himself. "Why would she want me, Fliss? I cannot provide the kind of life she is accustomed to." Even as he said it, he wondered if he were asking her about Beatrice, or about herself.

"Since you and Edmund are the only eligible men in the neighborhood, and Edmund favors Evangeline, Beatrice may be forced to see your merits."

"And if all she sees is my lack of wealth and station?"

She sighed. "I would love to promise you it won't come down to that, Silas, but I can't. It is the society we live in. We are quite the pair, aren't we? I cannot find anyone I wish to marry, and you have found someone you might marry and are afraid she will not return your feelings. Since you have no money, you will have to use your charm."

"You think I am charming?" he asked with a grin.

Ignoring his question, she paced back and forth, rubbing her hands on her upper arms. "Silas, have you done anything to see if there is a physical spark between you and Beatrice? Not kiss her, but let your hand linger on her arm? Brush away a strand of hair?" Felicity stopped pacing and faced him.

Despite the darkness of the room in the feeble candlelight, Silas spied a crumb on the corner of her mouth.

He shook his head. It had never occurred to him to try any of those things with Beatrice. And right now, that little crumb on Felicity's mouth was drawing all of his attention.

"I believe you should. When we return to Upper Pangford, we'll need to find an appropriate occasion." She tapped a finger against her lips.

Those lips. Why had he never noticed before how inviting they were? How kissable.

He wondered if she would feel a spark with him if he wiped that crumb away. Felicity was the only person he felt safe enough with to share his scars, his nightmares, his hopes. He cupped her chin in his hand, his thumb brushing the crumb from her lips.

It was such a simple interaction. A friendly gesture. Until it wasn't. Until he became aware of nothing more than the softness of her skin. The sparks that flew through his hand lit a fire inside him.

She grasped his wrist, and they stood still as if frozen in time. As his thumb traced her mouth, her lips parted, and he was overcome with the desire to kiss her.

"Do you do this with all the other girls?" Felicity said, her voice cracking.

Her eyes were shadowed pools, pools that he could drown in. "Do what? This?" He leaned toward her, his mouth hovering over hers. Her breath was warm against his mouth. Did he dare kiss her?

"Fliss?" he asked.

Her hand tightened on his wrist, pulling him closer.

He bent and pressed his lips against hers. She was so soft. Warm and inviting. She shivered at his touch, but she did not pull away.

He kissed her gently once. Twice. He slipped his arms around her waist, drawing her near, certain she could feel his heart pounding in his chest. All thoughts of anyone else fled. He was only aware of her in his arms, the way she fit against him. Her lips moved against his, hesitant at first, but growing in confidence. All the times he feared for his life in India melted away in her arms. Right now, here with her, he was safe.

It was the only place he wanted to be.

He broke off the kiss and pressed his cheek against her hair. He was about to speak when Felicity put her hands on his chest and pushed him away. She stared at him for a moment, her lips turned downward in a frown.

He lifted an errant strand of her hair and tucked it behind her ear. "Was I wrong to kiss you?"

"Silas," she said with a groan. "What are we doing? You are Edmund's friend. My friend. I wanted it to stay like that, the three musketeers, but that kiss.... Now you've gone and changed everything."

She picked up her candle and fled the room. His own candle flickered as she passed by him.

He was tempted to follow her upstairs but knew if he did, he would not be able to refrain from asking her if the world had stopped for her when he kissed her, the way it had for him. What if it hadn't? What if she hadn't felt the sparks that still lingered on his lips?

He shook his head as if by doing that, he could shake his thoughts of her away.

Chapter Fifteen

September 30, 1857

London, England

Felicity found it impossible to sleep. Every time she closed her eyes, she pictured people shouting at Silas and throwing rocks, his head cut open and bleeding. And when she opened her eyes, she felt his thumb brushing her lips. When he'd kissed her, she'd trembled all the way down to her toes.

She shivered. Her room was cold, but the real problem was that shivery feeling inside her that started with the kiss and hadn't left her. She burrowed under the blankets and tried to recall her favorite plants of the day. When that failed to distract her, she began a mental arrangement of everything in the conservatory, from the smallest plants to the bench and chairs. That usually calmed her mind, but not tonight.

Tonight, her thoughts refused to be tamed and, like a rogue on the loose, ran continually back to Silas and the warmth of his hand cupping her chin, his lips on hers. The roughness of his unshaven skin against her face.

The kiss was brought on by their familiarity. And by his vulnerability in telling her more about India. It was nothing more than that. It couldn't be more than that. But uncertainty seeped into her mind, seeping into her thoughts the same way the afternoon rain dampened her cloak. Maybe she had wanted that kiss. Maybe she had wanted it ever since he came back.

If that was true, she wasn't ready to admit it, because she didn't know what to do with those feelings. She tossed in the bed, unable to sleep. Tomorrow, she would have to share a carriage with Silas all the way back to Upper Pangford.

She sat upright on her bed. Would Edmund be able to tell that something had changed? How was she going to face Silas? And her brother? She flopped back down and pulled the pillow over her face. It would be so much simpler if he had never kissed her.

So much simpler if she hadn't wanted him to.

She fell asleep sometime before dawn and was awakened by the maid. "Miss Felicity, your brother is already at breakfast. He has sent for a carriage and wishes to leave London as early as possible."

Felicity rose and filled the basin. She splashed the cold water on her face, washing away any traces of sleep. She dressed and directed the maid to arrange her hair in a simple bun. When she reached the breakfast room she hesitated. Edmund's voice carried into the hallway, and she heard Silas responding.

The thought of their midnight interaction made her suddenly shy. She'd never been awkward around Silas, and she didn't like the idea of that changing now. She entered the breakfast room, and Silas sprang to his feet so quickly that his plate jostled his cup, spilling the contents onto the tablecloth.

Edmund laughed. "It's only Fliss! You would think the Queen herself had entered the room by your reaction. What has gotten into you?"

Felicity filled a plate and joined the men at the table. She kept her eyes on her food. She knew full well from her own failure to find rest that Silas had lingered downstairs when she went to bed. She'd heard his footsteps pause outside her door in the wee hours of the morning. Hesitantly, she lifted her eyes and saw the dark circles under his.

"Neither of you look like you slept," Edmund said. "What were you up to last night?"

"Nothing," Silas muttered.

Felicity took a bite of bread rather than answer.

"I slept as sound as ever," Edmund said. He raised another forkful of food to his mouth and chewed, his gaze darting between Silas and Felicity. "You've hardly touched your food, Silas. Aren't you hungry?"

Felicity fumbled her knife and it clattered to her plate. Silas jumped at the sound.

Edmund leaned back in his chair, folding his arms. "What aren't you telling me?"

Felicity's ears grew hot and she was sorry she hadn't chosen a hairstyle that concealed them. "We are eager to be back in Upper Pangford. Isn't that so, Silas?"

He dabbed his mouth with a napkin, reminding her of the way he touched her face last night. The same thought must have crossed his mind, for he set his napkin down and focused his gaze on his plate. "Yes, it will be good to be home," he muttered.

Nothing would be resolved until they had a chance to talk, and it was unlikely they would find an opportunity with Edmund around. She forced herself to eat something and then excused herself from the table to pack her things.

The footman handed Felicity into the carriage first. She chose the forward-facing bench seat and gave her hoop skirt a slight lift before sitting. Much to her annoyance, Edmund climbed in and sat across from her. Silas poked his head into the carriage and paused, indecision on his face.

"Sit across from me so I don't have to crank my head around to talk to you," Edmund said.

Felicity attempted to tuck her skirt out of the way as he sat beside her. No amount of tucking could keep the billowing bottom portion of her skirt from touching his leg. Edmund knocked on the ceiling of the carriage, and the driver set the conveyance in motion.

Edmund started a conversation with Silas about their schoolmates. Who had married, who had fallen on hard times, who was successful beyond anything they had imagined possible.

It was impossible for her to care about any of the gossip, but it was a welcome distraction. She stifled a yawn. The rocking motion of the carriage, combined with her fatigue from a sleepless night, soon got the best of her. Her eyes closed, and her chin dropped as she dozed off. The uncomfortable position caused her to awaken with a jerk. She fidgeted in her seat.

Edmund was now talking to Silas about things around the estate which was only slightly less tedious. She supposed it was good Edmund cared about such things since he was to inherit, but she imagined Silas was less than entertained by it. She glanced sideways as his gaze flicked over to her. Felicity rolled her eyes, and the awkwardness that had surrounded them at breakfast dissipated. Silas stifled a grin. Edmund, as usual, was oblivious to the silent exchange between the two of them.

Felicity fought to keep her eyes open but soon lost the battle and drifted off to sleep again. She awakened, warm and comfortable, with her cheek resting on...someone.

She was in the carriage.

And she heard Edmund's voice.

But it was not Edmund she was resting against.

She opened one eye, just a slit. Edmund was indeed sitting across from her, saying something about refreshing the horses.

She glanced down and saw a man's trousered leg resting near her skirt.

Silas.

She'd fallen asleep on Silas. Slowly, so as not to draw attention to that fact, Felicity straightened and opened her eyes. Edmund stopped talking and pointed to her face.

"You have wrinkles on your cheek," he said, with childish delight.

"If that is the only scar I bear from listening to your scintillating conversation then I have come out the victor," she said. Her cheek was damp, and she wondered in horror if she had drooled on Silas's arm. She retrieved the handkerchief tucked in her sleeve and dabbed at her face.

"I'll see to the horses," Edmund said.

"I'll come with you," Silas said.

Felicity followed them out of the carriage, hoping that getting some air would keep her awake for the rest of the journey. Judging by the sun, it was past noon. Her stomach rumbled, and she glanced at the inn, wondering if they should get some food while the horses rested.

They should be home in a little over two hours. Silas and Edmund spoke with the man attending to the horses and Felicity wandered off. It was good to stretch her legs. Though it was not raining, the air was chilly, and she drew her cloak around her. She paused to examine some bright red berries on a bush, wondering what sort they were, and if they were edible or poisonous. A little bird fluttered over and pecked at the berries. They must not be poisonous to birds.

Silas jogged over to her. "Edmund wishes to get something to eat. Are you hungry?"

She touched her cheek, self-conscious of the impressions on it from the fabric of his sleeve.

"It's nothing, Fliss," Silas said, as if he read her thoughts. "Edmund loves to tease you, you know that. Come." He offered her his arm, and she placed her hand through the crook of his elbow. Much to her relief, she did not detect any wet spots on his sleeve.

"I am envious you were able to sleep," Silas said.

She chuckled. "Thank you for keeping Edmund occupied so that I could rest."

"Perhaps you should return the favor on the rest of the journey," Silas said.

Felicity stopped. "You wish to sleep on my shoulder? I think you would get a crook in your neck."

"I wish to be where you are," Silas said, touching her gloved hand.

Felicity pulled away from him and tucked her hands beneath her cloak. "You mustn't say such things. Especially not when the whole purpose of having you on this outing was so you could spend some time with Beatrice."

Silas scuffed the ground with his boot. "Of course, Miss Wixom. I did not mean to make you uncomfortable."

Felicity sighed. "Miss Wixom? Is this how it is going to be between us?"

Silas shrugged. "You tell me. I shall do whatever it is that you wish."

She studied him, longing to say what was really going through her head. That she was glad he had finally opened up to her about India. That she couldn't stop thinking about that kiss. That she wished it had never happened and that things between them had not changed. But did she really wish he had never kissed her?

Things were so much simpler when they were children. Now everything between them was complicated. She wished she hadn't spent half the night re-living that kiss. It would be so much better if they had never become adults, never grown into so many rules and customs that stifled their interactions.

"I...," she began.

"Are you coming?" Edmund called.

Before she could answer, Silas stopped her. "Fliss, about last night in the kitchen..."

She moved away from him. "It never happened, Silas. We must put it behind us. Forget it as you have tried to forget India." The art school application weighed heavily on her mind. If she got in, she would leave Silas behind in Upper Pangford and go to London. It wasn't fair to get close to him when her intention was to leave everything behind. It was best to put the kiss behind her and let him get on with his life.

But that kiss.

When she'd asked Silas if he felt any spark for Beatrice, she had never imagined what that spark could be like. Her spine tingled thinking about his lips on hers.

But now what? She didn't want him to give his heart to her only for her to hurt him. He didn't deserve that.

The best thing to do was to deny she had any feelings for him. She must not give him false hope, must not confess her growing attachment to him, must never tell him that she wanted him to kiss her again. And again.

"We had bread in the kitchen, Silas. Promise me it will not be anything more."

He turned away from her, gazing at the horizon. "Is that what you want?"

She closed her eyes and swallowed hard. "It is what I need."

"Then I promise you I will not mention it again."

She hurried over to Edmund who handed her a paper-wrapped sausage roll. "You two were taking so long that I purchased some sausage for us to eat in the carriage. Otherwise, we shall never reach Upper Pangford before dinner."

"Do you only think about your stomach?" Silas asked, joining them. He did not meet Felicity's eyes.

Edmund grinned at him. "Food, and Miss Evangeline Harris."

When Silas got in the carriage, he sat next to Edmund, as far away from her as possible. Felicity stared out the window, pretending that she did not notice or care. Edmund prattled on about nothing as they journeyed, and she was grateful to let him carry the conversation while she paid little attention to the scenery going by.

The friendship was damaged and she didn't know how to repair it. If she succeeded in getting Beatrice to marry Silas, she would lose him. But if she went to art school, she would leave him behind. Either way, she would end up alone.

Her thoughts circled around and around, always coming to the same conclusion. If she cared about him at all, she must help him secure his own future and happiness. The remedy was clear--she had to let him go.

Chapter Sixteen

October 5, 1857

Upper Pangford, England

Silas fingered the invitation. It was from the Turners, inviting him to an evening of cards at their home this coming Saturday.

John peered over his shoulder. "Are we all invited?"

"You don't live here," Silas said. "Don't you have something to do at the vicarage?" The last thing he needed was to have his older brother scrutinizing his every move with the Turner family.

John sighed. "I am on my way back to the vicarage now. I only stopped by to see mother for a moment after I finished visiting the poor from my parish. It is a very big responsibility."

Silas snorted. He refused to feel sorry for John. "You have a home and income."

"Which is all the more reason I need to be out in society. I would like a wife to share it with," John said.

Silas sighed. "I cannot invite you to a private event in someone's home."

"Why are you invited?" John asked.

"I am acquainted with the oldest daughter, Miss Beatrice Turner."

John gripped his shoulders. "You're courting someone? Good for you! Does this mean that Miss Wixom is available? I always thought she would favor you."

Silas was taken aback. John with Felicity? While John was closer to her age than Mr. Woodburn, he couldn't picture her marrying his older brother. "Why would you think of Felicity?"

"I haven't found a wife in my own parish, so I am considering options in Upper Pangford. Louisa James and I do not get along. No one wants the burden of both Miss Eggleton and her overbearing mother, and you are courting Miss Turner. That leaves Felicity."

"You should have a conversation with her before you decide to court her. If she does not want to be a vicar's wife, it would save you a great deal of trouble to know that from the beginning."

John grunted. "Are you saying she would object to me?"

Silas thought about her letter months ago where she referred to John as a stick-in-the-mud. John might not be her first choice, but then again, he was eligible, respectable, and had a living at the vicarage. The only reason she would refuse him was if she did not love him.

"She knows her own mind, that's all," Silas said.

John studied him. "You know Felicity well. Are you sure Miss Turner is the right woman for you?"

Silas sighed. He was less certain of it all the time.

"I must return home," John said. "But I will make a stop along the way. I may see you on Saturday yet."

Silas saw him out and then sat in his father's study. His thoughts wandered. What if he had dared send Felicity the letter he wrote to her in India? Would things be different between them now? But he had not sent it, and now, he would never know.

If he wanted to hold onto their friendship, it was best to carry on as they had before the trip to Kew Gardens. Part of him knew he should regret that kiss, but another part of him knew he would treasure it forever.

October 10, 1857

Upper Pangford, England

When Saturday came, Silas arrived at the Turner home exactly on time. Mr. and Mrs. Turner greeted him warmly, but Beatrice was nowhere in sight. They directed him to the parlor where most of the guests were gathering. It was the first of three connecting rooms being used for this evening's party. Beyond the parlor, he saw tables in the drawing room, and further still, a room filled with greenery. He suspected couples would escape to that room for a little privacy during the evening.

Mr. and Mrs. Wixom were in one corner of the parlor with their daughter, Lucy. They were talking to Felicity's friend, Louisa. Edmund was standing not far from them talking to Evangeline and her parents. He scanned the room for Felicity and was relieved when he didn't see her.

He wandered over to the far room to see if Beatrice was awaiting him there. It was as if he'd entered a jungle. Plants were crammed into every corner, so crowded that he could hardly distinguish one from another. He wondered what Felicity would think of the arrangement. As if his thoughts had the power to conjure her, he heard her voice.

"If you'll excuse me, Mr. Woodburn, I must go to my family."

Silas peered around a tall, green plant that hid her from view. Mr. Woodburn was standing close to her, his rotund stomach straining the buttons on his waistcoat. His graying sideburns contrasted with his flushed cheeks,

"Your family is engaged in conversation, and your parents will not object to us spending a little time together here." The man took Felicity's hand and pulled her closer. "Let's take this opportunity to get to know one another."

Felicity tugged her hand out of his and stepped away, backing further into the corner. She had nowhere else to go, bounded on one side by a cascade of ferns and by Mr. Woodburn on the other.

Silas hesitated, wondering if he should intervene. Neither of them had noticed him yet.

"Don't be frightened, Miss Wixom. I only wish for us to become better acquainted. I am in need of a wife, you see, and the time is right for you to marry. I would provide you with a good home."

"You are mistaken, Mr. Woodburn. I have no immediate plans to marry. My art occupies much of my time, and I fear I will make a poor substitute for your late wife." Felicity raised her voice, and her eyes flitted about the room as if in search of rescue. Her gaze fell upon Silas, and she gave him a nod.

He strode forward. "Mr. Woodburn, how nice to see you. And you, Miss Wixom. Might I join you?" He tipped his hat.

Mr. Woodburn eyed him and grunted. "We are not in need of your company, sir."

Beatrice Turner entered the room. "There you are, Silas! I have been looking all over for you. You must come at once as we are about to start whist. You must be my partner."

She glanced at Mr. Woodburn and Felicity. "Would you care to join us?"

Before Mr. Woodburn could answer, John Parker strode across the room and offered his arm to Felicity. "I would love to join you," he said. "And Miss Wixom has consented to be my partner."

Felicity's mouth gaped open, but she recovered rapidly and took John's arm.

"What are you doing here?" Silas asked, surprised by his brother's sudden appearance.

"Mr. Turner and I met a few days ago and he invited me." He nodded at Beatrice. "Miss Turner, lovely to see you again."

Silas trailed after John and Felicity and they were all soon seated at a card table. John shuffled the deck and dealt out the cards.

"I don't know about you, Miss Wixom, but I have always been lucky at this game," he said.

Beatrice examined her hand and smiled. She led with the ace of spades, and on his turn, Silas played a lower card, giving her the trick. She started the next hand with the king of spades and managed to get John to play the queen. Once again, Beatrice took the hand.

"You may start using your luck at any time, Mr. Parker," Felicity said.

"I'm afraid I cannot control it like that," he said.

Silas stifled a laugh. He glanced at Felicity, expecting her to roll her eyes, but she did not look at him.

As the rounds continued, he became more and more distracted. He understood Felicity's humor better than John ever would. He knew which card she was about to play, without even seeing her hand. Couldn't she see he was a better match for her than his brother?

The game ended rather quickly, and he and Beatrice were victorious. Felicity rose from the table. "Thank you for the game, Mr. Parker."

"We must play another round, Miss Wixom, and redeem ourselves," John said.

"I'm afraid I am a poor partner tonight. I am feeling rather faint."

Before John could answer, Felicity left for the parlor.

"Oh dear, we need another player," Beatrice said, shuffling the cards.

Silas rose from the table. "I shall go in search of someone." He went directly to the parlor where he found Felicity in a quiet corner.

"How are you feeling?" he asked. "May I get you something?"

"What are you doing here? Shouldn't you be with Miss Turner?" she hissed.

"I had to know if you were truly ailing," he said.

"I am fine, Silas. I didn't feel like playing, that's all."

Edmund and Evangeline entered the room and went to the refreshment table. Beatrice soon joined them, scanning the room for Silas.

"Now you've done it," Felicity said. "You've left her to talk to me when I am in no need of your assistance. What will she think?"

Beatrice frowned at Silas and turned her attention back to Evangeline. "Mr. John Parker and I find ourselves alone at the card table. Will you and Mr. Wixom join us?"

Edmund and Evangeline agreed, and Silas watched helplessly as they left the room to play another round with John.

"She will think you've cast her aside," Felicity said.

"That was not my intent. What shall I do now?"

Felicity got to her feet. "I see my parents. I think I'll ask Mother to accompany me home. Will you tell Edmund to keep an eye on Lucy?"

"Please don't be like this. Are you still mad about London?"

"Mad that you made a mess of our friendship? Yes, I suppose I am."

He took her hand and she froze.

"Please tell me how to fix this," he said.

"Us? Or things with Miss Turner?" Her jaw was set, challenging him.

He wished someone would tell him the right thing to say, the right thing to do. Perhaps the best thing he could do for their friendship was give it some time. "With Miss Turner," he said.

She removed her hand from his grasp. "I shall buy some flowers tomorrow and you will take the bouquet to Miss Turner. You will apologize profusely and declare your love to her. That is how you fix this.

He was tempted to ask her if giving her flowers would fix things between the two of them, but he thought better of it. "Thank you. I'll see you tomorrow."

"Tomorrow I will buy the flowers. Come get the bouquet the next day."

"Shouldn't I see Beatrice as soon as possible to apologize?"

Felicity shook her head. "Give her time to miss you."

He nodded, wishing that kiss had not changed everything between them. Wishing she were his friend once again.

Chapter Seventeen

October 11, 1857

Upper Pangford, England

The October sunshine did little to warm the potting shed as Felicity worked to transfer a fern to a larger container. Her gloves sat on the table, and she knew Mother would scold her for not protecting her hands, but some tasks were better without the gloves. Having her hands in the soil grounded her.

Her work was interrupted by the butler, who appeared quite annoyed to have to come all the way out into the garden this fine afternoon.

"This came for you, Miss," the butler said, presenting the silver salver to her with a weathered, dirty card on top. She recognized it immediately. The bits of lace and ribbon she had glued on the card, the words copied carefully in her best hand.

It was the Valentine she'd sent to Silas months ago. Had it never reached India? Or had it arrived and never made its way to Silas?

She wiped her hands on her apron before picking up the stained card. One corner was ripped, and a bit of lace had come off. It had not fared well on its journey to India and back. She wondered how it had returned to her.

While playing whist on Saturday, she found herself constantly comparing Silas to his brother, John. Silas understood her. He made her laugh. The game with John only reinforced in her mind that she was more compatible with Silas. That had been the problem with every man who had shown interest in her the past three years. Without realizing it, she had compared them all to Silas, and they always came up short.

She was grateful he'd never received the Valentine now that he was seeing someone else. That little piece of her heart had come back into her possession. She carried the fern and the Valentine back to the house. Once the fern was settled in its place in the conservatory, she debated what to do with the card.

She went to the scullery to wash her hands, and gave the card to a maid. "This is rubbish. Please throw it away."

The maid read Silas's name on the card and raised an eyebrow at Felicity. "Did Mr. Parker send it back to you?"

"I don't believe it ever reached him, and as you can see, it is in no condition to give to him now."

"What is in no condition?" Edmund asked, as he entered the scullery.

"Nothing important." Felicity hung up her apron. "I must get to the flower shop."

"What are the flowers for this time?"

"Silas wants to send some to Beatrice."

"And you don't mind?"

"Why should I? I promised I would help him."

Edmund shook his head. "Sometimes I think that you and Silas...."

Lucy popped into the scullery. "There you are! I'm ready to go."

Edmund did not finish his sentence, and Felicity wondered what he was going to say. Were her feelings for Silas so obvious that even Edmund was aware of them?

"You'll be home for dinner, won't you?" Edmund asked.

"You worry like a mother hen," Felicity said. "We shall not delay your dinner. I know what truly matters to you."

He grinned at her and left the room.

Later that night, when her family had retired for the evening, Felicity fetched the flowers and two vases from the scullery and carried them to the warmth of the conservatory to work. She set everything on a small table and lit a few more candles before spreading out the flowers. She sorted them into two piles: one for the bouquet she would make tonight for herself, and one for the bouquet she would make for Silas to give to Beatrice tomorrow.

It was therapeutic to work with the yellow carnations and orange marigolds. She needed greenery. Basil grew in the conservatory year-round, and she cut some stems for her bouquet.

It was far better to work through her feelings here, in plant form, than to let anyone know her private thoughts. She would make the bouquet and enjoy it in her room until it died, and she would let her feelings die with it. She would not interfere with Silas's chance of happiness with Beatrice. He must never know of her attraction to him.

Felicity stomped her foot in frustration. She and Beatrice had become friends. Not as close as Felicity and Louisa, but she would never intentionally hurt Beatrice's feelings. Silas deserved someone who was intelligent and kind, like Beatrice. But she wished things were different. Their friendship would slip away once he was married, and she put all of her grief over that loss into the bouquet.

Felicity did not rush. The height of the carnations was visually pleasing in the vase. Yellow for disdain. She had only disdain for herself, for falling in love with Silas even as she helped him court someone else. It was insincere, the way she pretended to be happy for him as he worked to win Beatrice's heart, and she hated herself for lying.

She added marigolds around the carnations to represent her grief, but the bouquet still lacked something. She turned it around and considered her options. Wormwood.

She had one growing in the corner, and she cut a few fronds from the potted shrub. The leaves added texture to the arrangement, and bitterness. Her bitterness over what could never be.

Lastly, she added basil for hate. She didn't hate Beatrice. No one did. And she could never hate Silas. But she hated her own cowardice, her own lack of confidence. Her own fears.

Her bouquet needed one more thing—a ribbon.

Black, of course.

It was beautiful. If it weren't for all the meanings hidden within it, she would have shown it off proudly to friends and family. It was some of her very best work. But the bouquet, and her feelings, would remain hidden. It was best that way.

Felicity yawned. She had no idea how much time had passed. Pale moonlight filtered through the conservatory glass, giving the flowers an ethereal quality. She traced a finger gently over the petals and leaves, savoring the textures. The pungent scent of marigolds mingled with the spicy odor of the basil, and she inhaled deeply.

Silas was right. Flowers had their own beauty and should be appreciated for what they were. She thought of the cashmere shawl tucked upstairs, the one Silas had given her because it was the color of marigolds. She loved that marigolds reminded him of home, and that he associated the flower with happiness and not with grief. Perhaps flowers should have the meanings each person assigned to them individually.

Her eyelids were heavy as she finished, and she left the bouquet and the scraps of stems and leaves on the little table. She would have plenty of time in the morning to clean things up and to make the bouquet for Silas. She left the remaining flowers, the ones meant for Beatrice, in a jar of water.

Felicity went upstairs and didn't wake her maid to help her get ready for bed. She unpinned her hair and brushed it out herself. Securing it in a braid, she painstakingly undid the fastenings in her layers of clothing and slipped into her night dress. Her room was cold, especially in contrast to the warmth of the conservatory, and she shivered. Climbing into bed, she pulled the covers up to her chin.

She closed her eyes, picturing Silas as he had been at the Harvest Ball. His teasing smile. His unruly hair. His hands, so strong as they held hers.

October 12, 1857

Upper Pangford, England

She awakened to the draperies being opened, and light flooding the room.

"Time to get up, sleepyhead," Lucy said, sitting beside her on the bed. "Mother sent me to wake you and to see if you are well."

Felicity blinked and stifled a yawn. "I am fine."

She sat up, dreading placing her bare feet on the cold floor. The sooner she was dressed, the sooner she could go downstairs where it was warmer. An afternoon in the conservatory would be just the thing today.

The conservatory. The flowers.

"Lucy, I left a bouquet in the conservatory last night. Could you bring it to me?"

Lucy hurried off and Felicity went to the cupboard and selected a plain, gray dress to wear while she painted this afternoon. Perhaps Miss Dalrymple would bring her a new specimen. But if not, she wanted to revisit previous paintings and see if she could improve on them.

Lucy returned with a jar of roses.

"Not those," Felicity said. "The vase with the yellow carnations."

"These were the only flowers in the conservatory," Lucy said.

Felicity's heart sank faster than a stone on the River Pang. "What do you mean the vase isn't there? I left it on the table last night."

"See for yourself if you don't believe me," Lucy said.

Felicity raced down the stairs. Lucy followed. Once inside the conservatory, Felicity stopped short, panic flooding through her. "They were right here last night, on the table." Her scissors and bits of stems and leaves still remained, but there was no sign of the vase.

"Who has been in here? Edmund? Mother?"

"Silas came by earlier and was talking to Edmund about some flowers," Lucy said.

"How long ago?" Felicity grasped Lucy's shoulders.

"Ouch. You're hurting me."

Felicity released her. "When was Silas here?"

Lucy shrugged. "More than an hour ago."

Felicity ran for the door. She had to get to Silas, had to stop him from delivering the flowers. It was all a terrible mistake.

Lucy caught her before she went outside. "Let me fix your hair. And you need shoes. You can't run through the neighborhood like this."

Felicity allowed Lucy to take her upstairs, brush out her hair, and secure it in a bun. Her reflection was pale in the mirror, her face drawn with worry. Her first inclination was to reach Silas. But Lucy said he'd come more than an hour ago.

"It's too late," she whispered. "I've ruined everything."

Lucy knelt on the floor beside her and clasped her hands. "Tell me."

"That bouquet," Felicity said as tears fell. "Silas has taken it to give to Beatrice, and he'll never forgive me."

"He took carnations and marigolds to Beatrice? Are you daft? Why would you make those for him?"

"Silas was meant to take the roses. That bouquet was for me."

Felicity wiped her eyes and blew her nose. She must try to repair what she had done. She couldn't face Silas yet, could not face his disappointment in her, the betrayal he must feel. No, first she would go to Beatrice.

Chapter Eighteen

October 12, 1857

Upper Pangford, England

The carriage stopped before the Turner home, and the footman opened the door. Felicity inhaled deeply, as if she could draw courage from the crisp, autumn air. She gathered her cloak about her and stepped from the carriage. The doors of the Turner home loomed large and filled her with foreboding.

"Miss Wixom, shall we wait here?" the footman asked.

Felicity nodded. "I shall not be here long."

She walked up the steps and knocked. An eternity passed before the door creaked open and the butler greeted her. She went inside and handed her cloak, hat, and gloves to a waiting maid with some reluctance. If she had to leave the house in a hurry, she would not be able to easily retrieve them.

The maid showed her into a parlor where she did not take a seat but waited anxiously for Beatrice to arrive.

"Felicity." Beatrice rushed over and clasped her by the hands. "Your hands are like ice. I'll have the maid bring something hot to drink."

Felicity shook her head. "I cannot stay long, but I have a matter of some importance to discuss with you."

Beatrice frowned and led Felicity to a pair of chairs. "You look so serious. What is wrong?"

Beatrice's eyes were warm and trusting, adding to Felicity's misery. "I have made a grave error," she said. "I must assure you that I never meant for this to happen, for you to get hurt."

Confusion flitted across Beatrice's face. "What do you mean?"

Felicity sighed. "I must start at the beginning. As you know, I have a long acquaintance with Mr. Silas Parker."

Beatrice leaned back in her chair. "I am aware. If you have come on his behalf, I do not wish to discuss it."

Felicity rose and paced the room. "Please let me explain. When Silas...Mr. Parker...returned from India, he asked me to help him find a suitable match, and I introduced you. He is disastrous when it comes to flowers and their meanings, so I helped him with the bouquets he sent you and I encouraged him to also send you notes, and to visit."

"*You* sent the bouquet?" Beatrice asked, her voice hardened.

"I did make the bouquet, but not for you."

"Who was it for?"

Felicity sighed and sat back down. "It was for me. I was upset and I poured my feelings into that bouquet. I was not awake when Mr. Parker came to get the flowers for you. You were supposed to get roses, and I'm sorry. Please don't blame him. It was all a misunderstanding, and I never meant for anyone to be hurt."

"You put together those flowers?" Beatrice asked.

"Yes."

"For yourself?"

"Yes," Felicity said.

Beatrice tilted her head downward, studying her hands in her lap.

Felicity waited, hoping Beatrice would say something. Anything would be better than this silence that hung thick in the room like a dense fog rolling in from the river. If Beatrice didn't speak in the next few minutes, Felicity would slip outside, never to return. Beatrice made a noise. A choked, strangled sort of noise.

Then she erupted, not in a torrent of tears or an angry tirade as Felicity expected, but in a burst of laughter. Loud and unladylike. Beatrice covered her mouth, her whole body shaking as a tear slipped down her cheek.

"You?" Beatrice gasped. "While I thought it out of character that Mr. Parker would bring such a bouquet to me, I would never have guessed that you were capable of creating such a menacing arrangement." Her laughter subsided to giggles as she struggled to catch her breath. "It was brilliant, those flowers. I am relieved to know that they were not intended for me."

Beatrice's reaction caught Felicity off guard, and she didn't know what to do next. Did this mean Beatrice would forgive Silas? If so, her mission had been a success. "Can you forgive him?"

Beatrice leaned forward and took one of Felicity's hands. "Whatever possessed you to make such a thing?"

Felicity bit her lip. She must never let it be known that she cared for Silas. If reconciliation between him and Beatrice was possible, she would do all within her power to facilitate it. He deserved happiness, and she still believed he and Beatrice were a good match. The reasons for the bouquet must forever remain a secret. "It was an upsetting day, that's all. I made the bouquet to express my emotions. No one was ever meant to see it. I planned to make a different bouquet for you out of roses, but I slept late and Silas took the wrong flowers."

"At first I was hurt," Beatrice said. "I thought he was trying to tell me he loathed me. But the flowers were so beautiful, I am sorry I threw them at him. I believe you when you say that he does not understand the meaning. What I don't understand is why you are helping him to court me."

"He's my friend. I would do anything for him. I must go," Felicity said. She couldn't be in the room any longer. She must get out of the way and let things between Beatrice and Silas run their natural course. She'd had enough of meddling in other people's romances. Enough of trying to arrange things so their lives would flow together.

If she got accepted into art school, it would not sting nearly as much when Edmund married Evangeline and Silas married Beatrice. She found no fault in any of them, and she wished them all happiness. But that did not mean she needed to stay in Upper Pangford while their lives moved on and she remained alone.

"Felicity, I must ask you," Beatrice said softly. "Did you make that bouquet for yourself because of your own feelings for Silas?"

Felicity fidgeted with the hem of her sleeve. She had rejected Silas's advances too many times, and she could not admit now that she regretted that. The truth would only make things worse. She would have to learn to live with regret.

"When you left the whist table," Beatrice said, "he went after you. He said he was looking for new players, but I saw him. He went directly to you. I see the way he looks at you, Felicity. Surely you have seen it. He lights up whenever he sees you. It was clear at Kew Gardens that you were very much on his mind."

"But you are perfect for him," Felicity said.

"I am not. Silas is a gentleman, and very handsome, and I was flattered by his attention. When he brought the bouquet, I was surprised and hurt, but I was also surprised by how quickly my feelings recovered. I am not upset at losing him, which tells me he was not the one for me. You should tell him how you feel."

Felicity rose from the chair. "I have made him angry. Even if I could find the courage to tell him, I don't think I can repair what I have done."

"He has always been your friend, and you have been his. It may not be easy to repair things between you, but you must summon the courage to try," Beatrice said.

When Felicity arrived home, the butler hurried to greet her. "Miss Wixom, there is a rather large delivery for you," he said. "I am having everything put in the conservatory."

The plants had arrived. She could postpone her conversation with Silas a bit longer. Once in the conservatory, she directed servants to bring supplies from the potting shed while she examined the new arrivals.

The tropical ti plants were even more beautiful than she had expected with their red-streaked leaves. The orchids were breathtaking, blooms of deep purple and delicate pink all at their peak.

Once she'd taken inventory of the delivered items, she dove into the project with renewed energy. Working in the dirt, separating roots, watering, trimming leaves, re-potting, and lifting or dragging containers around the conservatory soothed her. This was all she needed. While flowers had been her undoing with Silas, this batch of plants would redeem her during the garden tour.

Chapter Nineteen

October 12, 1857

Upper Pangford, England

S ilas opened the conservatory door and entered the room, carrying the bouquet of yellow carnations and marigolds. He hesitated for a moment, hurt and confusion swelling inside him. He'd never dreamed Felicity could do something so...cruel...as to create that bouquet. It was not like her.

That was why he was here. To see if she had an explanation. He went to her and set the flowers down on the table. "Why did you do it?"

She picked up a marigold and twirled it in her fingers. "Marigolds for grief. A black ribbon. I never thought you would choose the wrong flowers, Silas. These were never meant for you to give to Beatrice. I'm so sorry."

"I only saw the beauty of the arrangement. And I trusted you. When Beatrice made me leave and threw those flowers at me, it was humiliating."

She set the flower down and reached for his hand, but he withdrew. "It was a misunderstanding."

"A misunderstanding? I think we all understand the meaning of these flowers." He turned to leave.

"Please, don't go," she said. He sighed and sat in one of the chairs.

"I know I can't fix this. I know I can't make it right. I'm sorry, Silas So very sorry. Those flowers were not meant for Beatrice. I got the roses for her. This bouquet...these flowers were for me."

"For you?"

"Yes," she said, fingering the blossoms. "I disdain myself for being duplicitous. For helping you court someone else when I could not admit my own feelings for you. Hate and bitterness for my lack of courage in telling you."

"What are you saying, Felicity? You have made it clear to me again and again that all you want from me is friendship. You encouraged me to court Miss Turner. Why? Because I was not good enough for you? Because I can never be anything except your brother's friend?" He plucked a leaf of basil and crushed it, the scent filling the room.

Her cheeks flushed. "I convinced myself that you would never see me as anything but Edmund's little sister with skinned knees. I was so worried about you in India, but I couldn't admit to myself that my feelings had changed, so I refused all of your advances. I was so relieved when you came home safe that I promised myself I would help you find happiness with someone worthy of you. I should have been honest with you and with myself, but I was not. And now I regret it."

He leaned forward with his elbows on his knees, hands clasped together, his gaze fixed on the ground. Was she saying that she cared for him? That was what he'd been longing to hear from her, but now that she was finally saying it, he had trouble believing her. He got to his feet. "Thank you for your honesty. Enjoy the flowers."

He almost made it to the conservatory door before she ran after him and grabbed his hand. "Silas, please. What happens now?"

One question still hung between them, and he had to ask it. "If you get accepted to art school, will you go? Will you leave Upper Pangford behind?"

"I don't know, Silas. I haven't dared consider that I would get in. The garden show is in a few days, and my thoughts have been occupied with that." She let go of his hand. "I'm sorry I don't have a better answer for you."

He brushed her cheek with his fingertips. "Don't worry, Felicity. Enjoy your garden show. We both have decisions to make, and we'll sort it all out later."

He left her alone in the conservatory and exited the house, still unsettled. It was a fine night, and he didn't mind walking the short distance to his own home. He hadn't gotten very far down the drive when Edmund called after him. He was tempted to ignore him, but Edmund was persistent.

"Are things better between you and Fliss?" Edmund asked.

Silas shook his head. "I am afraid we are growing up in surprisingly painful ways. The three musketeers are no more."

"Maybe this will help," Edmund said, pulling something dirty and crumpled from his pocket. He handed it to Silas. "You should have this. She made it for you and sent it to India, but somehow it came back to her."

Silas took it from Edmund and smoothed it out. One of Felicity's handmade Valentines with ribbon and lace, and written in her neat handwriting: *I would not wish any companion in the world but you.*

"What's it from?" Edmund asked.

"Shakespeare. *The Tempest*, I believe. Where did you get this?"

"She threw it in the rubbish, and I fished it out. She always sent you Valentines, and you should have it."

It was ragged. And dirty. He could see why she threw it away. But he folded it gently and tucked it in his pocket.

"You and Fliss...you are meant to be together."

Silas stopped on the gravel drive. "How can you say that? I was at the meeting where your father discussed her marriage settlement. If I go to him, he will think I am after her money, and he will refuse me."

Edmund laughed. "You are mistaken. You have been part of the family for so long, it is not you he worries about when it comes to Felicity's inheritance."

Silas put his hands on his hips. "Really? What would your father say if I asked for her hand?"

Edmund placed his hand on Silas's shoulder. His face was serious. "My father would say that it took you far too long to come to your senses."

Silas could hardly believe it. Was Edmund right? The Wixoms had never given him any reason to feel inferior. He had done that all on his own. "And what do you think your sister would say?"

Edmund shrugged. "Felicity may be harder to convince, but you are a musketeer. I have every confidence in you."

As Silas walked home alone, excitement grew within him. The only obstacle that stood in the way of him proposing to Felicity was art school. He would never deny her that opportunity. But if she was in art school, he would want to be near her, where he could support her and watch her bloom.

Chapter Twenty

October 17, 1857

Upper Pangford, England

"The garden is a triumph, my dear," Miss Dalrymple said. "Your plant selection and the way you have them arranged is exquisite. I doubt anyone else on the tour will be able to compare."

"Thank you, that is very kind," Felicity said. But even after all her work, she saw things she would change.

She circled the room with Miss Dalrymple, commenting on orchids, ferns, ti plants, the orange tree, and more. "I have a surprise for you," Miss Dalrymple said.

"More plants? I think I have run out of space," Felicity said.

"No plants for now." She turned toward the drawing room, and through the glass doors, Felicity saw servants scurrying around setting her drawings and paintings on several easels in the room.

"No, I can't bear to have people see them," Felicity said. She moved toward the door. "I must stop them."

"Whatever for?" Miss Dalrymple asked. "You have produced some astounding work, and it should be displayed. I had to talk your father into it, but I think he will be quite pleased."

Felicity left the glassed-in conservatory and stopped in the center of the drawing room. Turning slowly, she took in her paintings: pale blue forget-me-nots, yellow and orange marigolds, the white and purple orchid, and more. She had never seen them displayed together this way, and it was overwhelming. While she was proud of what she had accomplished, knowing other people would see her work tonight left her feeling vulnerable. Exposed.

"Isn't it wonderful?" Miss Dalrymple asked. "I shall be back this evening."

Felicity sketched in her room, giving her hands something to do while she waited for the garden tour to begin. A knock at the door interrupted her. "Are you ready for me to help you dress?"

All of her work was on display tonight. All of her hopes and dreams, culminating in one evening. Tonight, she would not stand alone on the fringe of everything. Tonight would be her night, and tonight, she would shine.

Felicity pointed to her blue dress. "That one, I think. With the shawl from India."

"Yes, Miss," the maid said, and Felicity heard the approval in her voice.

As visitors filled the house that evening, they wandered past her paintings in the drawing room on their way to the conservatory. Felicity observed their faces carefully for their reactions. Much to her relief, she saw only smiles, nods, and pleasant conversations. Satisfied, she left her paintings and entered the conservatory, much more confident in her choice of plants.

Louisa was the first to greet her. "It's beautiful, Felicity. Your artistry is evident at every turn. I suspect you will be the envy of every housewife, and I would not be surprised if a few ask you to share your expertise in upgrading the plants in their own homes."

Felicity gave Louisa a hug. "Do you think so?"

Her friend nodded. "After tonight, you will be the talk of Upper Pangford. And your paintings are exquisite. Miss Dalrymple tells me she intends to publish some of your drawings and paintings in her new botany book. You shall be too busy to help me find a match," Louisa said.

"You will no doubt be better off on your own when it comes to finding a match, but I shall always have time for you."

Louisa linked her arm through Felicity's. "I will be grateful for your help, even if you only meet my prospective suitors and warn me away from the worst of them."

"That I can do. Come see my favorite ti plant." She turned abruptly and ran into a striking woman with two children in tow.

"I beg your pardon," Felicity said.

The woman's blond hair was pulled back from her face, ringlets falling down her back. The girl was a miniature version of her mother, while the boy, several inches taller than his sister, was scanning the crowd with serious eyes.

The woman touched the shawl on Felicity's shoulders. "You must be Felicity."

"Yes. And you are?"

The boy shouted "Silas!" and darted across the room.

His mother watched him go. She clasped Felicity's hand. "My name is Sarah Talbot. It is so nice to meet you. I am afraid we are at your party uninvited. I have come to see Mr. Parker, and Charlie has found him."

"How do you know my name?"

Mrs. Talbot smiled. "The shawl, my dear. I gave it to Mr. Parker to give to you upon his return. Might I surmise, since you are wearing it, that you and Mr. Parker have come to an understanding?"

"Not yet," Felicity said, bewildered that Silas had discussed her with this stranger.

"Silas worked for my husband, and when the mutiny began in India, he saved my life. He got me and my children out of the city and helped us get to Karnal. While we had the chance to pack a few belongings, Mr. Parker had only one possession with him: a letter from you. You sent him forget-me-nots, and I told him the woman who sent those flowers must surely care for him."

"Forget-me-nots are from our childhood," Felicity said. "Did he tell you?"

"They may be a childhood connection, but I think you sending them was something more. Was I mistaken?"

Felicity thought back on pressing those flowers. Mrs. Talbot was not wrong. Whether in a letter or in a Valentine, they had always been meant for Silas. He came toward them, the little boy pulling him by the hand.

"Mrs. Talbot," he said with a bow. "How good it is to see you and Charlie." He crouched down to eye-level of the girl. "Hannah, has Marietta made the journey from India with you?"

The girl nodded solemnly. "Mother made me leave her at the hotel tonight. She said Marietta was a bit under the weather and shouldn't come."

Silas nodded gravely. "Tell her that I send her my best wishes."

Silas was good with these children, but it didn't surprise her. He had always been so good to her, even when she was a child.

"And Mr. Talbot?" Silas asked. His face was strained and Felicity sensed his dread at hearing the answer. Was Mr. Talbot one of the casualties of the uprising?

To her relief, the woman smiled and gestured across the room where a distinguished looking gentleman was talking to Silas's father.

"He is here with us. We are going to settle in London, but I had to find you first."

Relief washed over Silas's face.

Felicity's presence was not needed at this reunion. "Please excuse me, Mrs. Talbot. I must see to the other guests."

"Wait," Mrs. Talbot said. Mr. Talbot was crossing the room. "You must not go yet. I want you to meet my husband."

When Mr. Talbot joined them, he clasped Silas in a hug. "I can never repay you for what you have done for my family."

"It is good to see you. How did you escape?" Silas said.

"I was able to make it home in the chaos, and our servants hid me for a few days. Then they helped me find a way to Meerut and from there, I rejoined Mrs. Talbot in Karnal."

Mrs. Talbot introduced her, and Mr. Talbot bowed, his face grave. "You are the one Mr. Parker could not get off his mind. I was not surprised when I heard he left the East India Company to return home to you."

"I did not know that," Felicity said, eying Silas.

The pulse in his temple throbbed, and he glanced at his feet.

Mr. Talbot said. "I believe he could sense, as I do, that the British government will be replacing the East India Company as the authority there. I am starting a new venture here, and I would like to ask Mr. Parker to consider working for me. If you have a moment, I'd like to discuss it with you."

"Of course," Silas said. The men excused themselves and left the conservatory.

Mrs. Talbot touched her arm. "I am happy to see Mr. Parker looking so well. His scar has healed quite nicely. Has he said much to you about India?"

"He has told me a little. I think India has haunted him, but seeing you and your family has lifted his spirits," Felicity said.

"He is a hero. Without his guidance, we would have gone to the Main Guard, and we may not have survived." She gestured at the plants surrounding them. "Are you responsible for all of this?"

Felicity flushed. "Yes."

"And your paintings are quite beautiful. You have a gift that should be utilized," Mrs. Talbot said.

"Thank you," Felicity replied. Mrs. Talbot took the children to join her husband. Felicity glanced around for someone to talk to and found Beatrice Turner heading her way.

"My aunt is thrilled with your garden and with your paintings," Beatrice said. "What an amazing evening. And to think, I was there when she first met you and proposed working together. You should be quite proud of yourself."

Felicity thanked her. It was very gracious of Beatrice to be so kind. To her surprise, John Parker joined them.

"Miss Wixom, it is good to see you again," he said. He turned to Beatrice. "And you, also, Miss Turner."

Beatrice took John's arm. "If you will excuse us, Felicity, I would like to talk to Mr. Parker about charity work in his parish. I have missed those opportunities since I left London."

Felicity returned to the drawing room where Miss Dalrymple introduced her to a handful of fellow-botanists and at least one botanical artist. Her head was spinning by the end of the evening, and she retreated to the conservatory for some peace and quiet.

She went to the sitting area where two letters rested on the little table, both addressed to her. She picked them up and took them to her room to read.

In the solitude of her bedroom, Felicity opened the letter from Silas and was surprised by the date. Silas had written this only a week after the mutiny in India. Had he kept the letter with him this whole time? She read the first part quickly, smiling as he mentioned the forget-me-nots and their childhood bond. As she continued reading, however, she slowed her pace.

If I survive this experience and return to England, I believe I may become a solicitor. It is not the most prestigious of jobs, but I find the work to be interesting.

I will never be able to provide the life that you are accustomed to, Felicity. I shall never be worthy of you. But we have been friends for many years, and if I make it out of here, I would like to court you.

If you are otherwise engaged, I shall step aside. But if you are unattached, Fliss, what do you think?

Ever your friend,

Silas

Beneath the letter, he had written more. The ink was different, and she suspected he had added this right before delivering it to her.

You have always been there to encourage me and to make me smile. Whether we are skipping stones or teasing Edmund, I always enjoy your company. I love your courage, your wit, and your artistic skill. You are a loyal, steady friend and you never fail to warm my heart. You are marigolds, orange blossoms, forget-me-nots, and all that is beautiful.

I would like to see our friendship grow into the kind of love that I now know I desire.

If you will have me, I will wear out my life seeing to your happiness.

Your most hopeful companion,

Silas

Why had Silas kept this from her until now? If he felt this way about her, why had he ever agreed to court Beatrice? Silas had given her many opportunities to make her feelings known, and she had failed to tell him every single time. She thought back to the dinner when he first returned from India, when he had held her hand beneath the table, and to the Harvest Ball when he danced with her in his arms. And when he'd kissed her after Kew Gardens, her response was to tell him he'd changed everything. How had she been so blind?

When she saw him again, she would make her feelings clear to him, for they were finally clear in her own mind. Dear Silas.

How she loved him. She set the letter on her bed and fingered the reply from the art school. Did she dare open it? Her hands trembled as she broke the wax seal and unfolded the letter.

Dear Miss Wixom,

Before we make a decision regarding your enrollment at the Female Academy of Art, we would like to see more of your work. Please arrange a time to bring your paintings to London at your earliest convenience. We look forward to evaluating your work.

The school had not said yes, but they had not said no, either. She lay back on her bed and closed her eyes. Was it possible that in the new year she would be living in London and focusing on her art? What would that mean for her and Silas?

Chapter Twenty-One

❀

October 28, 1857

London, England

When Silas arrived outside the Female Academy of Art building, he saw Felicity enter, carrying a large satchel. He had no idea how long she would be, or if the people she was meeting would make a decision about her enrollment today, or if they would let he know at a later date.

He paced outside, his nerves mounting. He patted his waistcoat to make sure the items he brought were still tucked safely in his pocket. No matter what happened between them today, he was determined to say what he had come all the way to London to say to her.

When she left the building, Silas could not read her expression. Her satchel appeared full, which meant she still had her portfolio with her. She walked down the steps and paused when she reached the street.

Silas approached her. "What did they say?"

She whirled around and stared at him. "What are you doing here?"

"Edmund told me where to find you," he said.

"Were you in London on business?"

He shook his head. "I came to see you. I have something to tell you."

"Something you couldn't say in Upper Pangford?"

"I didn't want to wait any longer," he said. "But first tell me, what did you find out from the school?"

"I got in," she said.

A grin spread across his face, and he swept her off the ground and spun her around while she laughed. "Congratulations!" He set her down and took a step back. Felicity's smile was more genuine than he had seen in a long time. "What does your father say?"

"He has agreed to it. I have Miss Dalrymple to thank for that. The response to my work during the garden tour convinced him."

"When do you begin?"

"Not until mid-January," she said. "I shall be in Upper Pangford until then. That will let us resolve things between us, will it not?"

"We don't need more time," he said. "We can resolve things today."

She frowned. "Right here? On the street? I suppose it will only take a moment for you to tell me you are going to become a solicitor and I can tell you I shall be an artist. Is that it? Are we going to leave it at that?"

"You are already an artist," Silas said. He withdrew the tattered Valentine and held it out to her.

"I threw that away," she said, wrinkling her forehead. "Where did you get it?"

"Maybe it was always meant to find its way to me."

She gave him a gentle shove. "When did you become such a romantic?"

"Ah, you finally see. I have always been this way."

"You have not," she said.

"Then perhaps it was you who was the romantic."

"Never," she scoffed.

He pulled out more Valentines and held them out for her inspection. She leaned forward, touching the edges, her face flooding with recognition.

"Are these the ones I sent you when you were at school?" she asked.

He nodded.

"You kept them."

"Every single one. I left them safe at home when I went to India, and now, this one joins them."

She held his gaze, her blue eyes unflinching. "I can't believe you kept these. They are the art and sayings of a child."

"All the better to bribe you with," Silas said.

"You almost had me convinced you were the romantic, but if you are to use them for blackmail, then I see that this cannot be the case."

"I shall return them to you if you wish," he said, holding them out.

She shook her head. "They were meant for you."

He tucked the Valentines back inside his waistcoat. "I shall hang onto them. They are fond memories for me, and I will need something to warm my heart when I am old and gray."

"You will have someone to warm you, Silas. I am sure of that."

It was now or never. He must tell her of his feelings before the moment was lost to him.

"Felicity. Fliss, if you are not the perfect match for me, then no one is. I have known that for a long time now. I first admitted it to myself in India, and I meant to send you a letter then, but I let fear govern me."

"The letter that you left in the conservatory?" she asked.

He nodded, reaching for her hand.

She let him take it. "What were you afraid of?"

He gave her a wry smile. "I was afraid of losing you. I am in love with you, Felicity Wixom, and I do not wish to hide that anymore. If you don't feel the same, tell me. I trust you to be honest with me, and if you wish for me to go away and never speak of these things again, I will abide by your wishes. Tell me, Fliss, do you love me?"

Her eyes shone, and he tried to memorize every freckle, every eyelash, everything about her face. He wanted more than Valentines cards to remember her by. He wanted all the memories he could hold. Her laughter, her blue eyes. He wanted a lifetime of them.

"Oh, Silas," she said. She dropped her portfolio case and wrapped her arms around him. "I think I have been in love with you since you pulled me from the River Pang when we were children, but I never dared believe you could love me, too."

He cupped her cheeks in his hands, tipped her face toward him, and kissed her. Gently at first, a question on his lips.

She tightened her hold on him and kissed him back, her lips forming the answer. Still in his arms, she whispered, "What do we do now?"

"I shall court you," he said, kissing her forehead and her cheeks before finding her mouth once again.

She laughed. "I believe courtship is for two people to get to know one another, and I think we already know each other very well."

"Then I shall ask your father for your hand." He nuzzled her neck and inhaled, drawing in the smell of her. Lavender, a hint of rosemary, and paint.

"Don't you think you should ask me first?"

He laughed. "Felicity Wixom, will you marry me?"

"Yes," she said, resting her cheek against his chest. "I'm sorry it took me so long to see how much I love you."

"Don't apologize," he said, kissing the top of her head. "You were worth the wait."

"Where will we live, Silas? What will we do?"

"I will be working with Mr. Talbot in London," Silas said. "I've found a small house to let, and you shall go to art school."

"You've thought of everything," she said. "Mrs. Felicity Parker. I like the sound of it."

"Will you be happy? Even if we are poor?" He wanted to make certain she considered the cost of marrying him.

"Even if we are as poor as church mice. But we won't be. At least, *I* won't be. I have a marriage settlement, remember?" she teased. "But you will have your work, and it will be enough."

"And the conservatory? You once told me that you would never leave it."

She planted kisses on his cheeks, his chin, and finally his lips. "Don't be silly. Edmund is forever in my debt for helping him to win over Evangeline. He will always welcome us back. Besides, he will be lonely without two of the three musketeers. I think he will be happy to have us visit as often as we like."

Silas picked up her portfolio and offered her his arm. "Where shall I escort you?"

"I shall go wherever you go, Silas. I am never going to lose you again."

Epilogue

❁

February 14, 1858

Upper Pangford, England

I t surprised Felicity as she stood in the church next to Silas that she was so nervous. After all, she had known him for so long. Family and friends had gathered this Sunday morning to witness their vows: Mother, Father, Silas's family, Lucy, Edmund and his new wife, Evangeline. She had no reason to have a case of nerves, yet her hands trembled.

It was the excitement of marrying her best friend, she decided, that made her tingle from head to toe. She had loved him from the moment he gave her a forget-me-not when she was eight years old, first as a friend, and now as her husband.

She wore a headpiece of myrtle and orange blossoms, and the delicate scent filled the air around her. Dressed in white, she stood beside Silas, who was handsome in his black coat.

When they had gone to meet with her parents about their engagement, Mr. and Mrs. Wixom had blessed the match.

"Why, then, did you work so hard to get me to marry Mr. Woodburn?" Felicity asked Mother.

"You have always been of your own mind," Mother replied. "I hoped if you thought we wanted you to marry someone else that you would finally see what was right in front of you all along."

After weeks of waiting and planning, the day was finally here.

They made their vows in the church in Upper Pangford, and afterward, headed back to Ashwick Manor to celebrate with their families. Felicity smiled until her cheeks ached, accepting congratulations and making conversation. Silas smiled at her from across the room. He made his way to her.

"Meet me in the conservatory," he said, and slipped away from the drawing room.

She followed him, and once inside, she took his hat and ruffled his hair.

He caught her wrist and kissed her palm. "I have a surprise for you. Close your eyes."

She did as he requested, and he guided her across the room. "Open them."

On the little table sat a pot of delicate blue flowers in bloom.

"Forget-me-nots in February? How?" She fingered the flowers gently.

"I have my secrets," Silas said. "Here."

She opened the card where he had written:

Roses are for love

Violets say be true

But forget-me-nots always

Remind me of you.

"You made me a Valentine?" she asked.

He nodded. "I don't have your skills, but I don't think it is terrible considering it is my first one."

"I love it," she said. She placed her hands behind his neck, pulling him close. "Will you always be my Valentine?"

His lips hovered above hers. "Always," he said, and he kissed her.

Historical Notes

Dear Reader,

I have done my best to be accurate in my portrayal of historical events in this novella. While studying political science in college, I took a South Asia politics class where we covered the uprising against the British in India. Since it happened during the Victorian era, I decided to use it as a backdrop in Forget-Me-Nots for Felicity. If you want to read more on this subject, I highly recommend *The Great Mutiny: India 1857* by Christopher Hibbert.

After the "Great Mutiny" in 1857, the British government essentially disbanded the East India Company and took control until India gained independence in 1947. Before that, the East India Company functioned as a pseudo-government entity with its own military (often British officers over soldiers comprised of men from the local communities).

Brigadier Graves and Captain Tytler are real people who I fictionalized in my story. The Brigadier was concerned that Captain Tytler's infantry would attack once they left Flagstaff Tower, but Tytler's men proved to be loyal. The British did detonate everything at the munitions building as they lost control of Delhi. I have adjusted the timeline and compressed some events to fit my fictional narrative.

Felicity and Silas's hometown, Upper Pangford, is a fictional village in Berkshire, England. on the River Pang. It is near Pangbourne and Reading.

Kew Gardens was greatly expanded and enhanced during 1857. At the time of this novel, the Palm House was in existence. The Eastern Cape giant cycad that Felicity views is still on display at the Palm House, and has been for 240 years. It is the oldest potted plant in the world.

Felicity applies to the fictional Female Academy of Art in the novella as art education for women was limited in Victorian England. The Society of Female Artists (now the Society of Women Artists) is a real organization and held their first art show in June of 1857. While two women helped found the Royal Academy of Art in1768, and women could exhibit in its annual Summer Exhibition, women were not allowed into their school until 1860 when Laura Herford applied with a drawing signed with only her initials and was accepted. Women, however, could not attend life drawing classes until 1890.

About the Author

Amy Newbold enjoys writing sweet, clean romances and the occasional ghost story. She learned to read at age four and has been reading and writing ever since. Her favorite thing about writing romance is capturing the spark of falling in love on the written page. Amy loves traveling, playing board games, birding, and spending time with her family. She has a deep appreciation for chocolate and is living her own happily ever after with her husband, artist Greg Newbold.

Stay in touch! If you would like to receive updates on new releases, book recommendations, insights into upcoming projects, and more, subscribe to my free newsletter : https://subscribepage.io/FGApSB

You may also subscribe on my website: https://www.amynewbold.com/

Also By Amy Newbold

Sweet & Clean Historical Romance

Amidst Ruins and Remembrances (Victorians at the Beach)
A Lady Most Alluring: A Grimm Regency Tale

Clean Contemporary

Ghosts of Grayhaven (with Lark Wright)

Picture Books

If Picasso Painted a Snowman
If Da Vinci Painted a Dinosaur
If Monet Painted a Monster

For more information about Amy's books, visit: https://www.amynewbold.com/

Acknowledgements

Special thanks to my critique partners and beta readers who helped me make this story so much better: Lark, Michelle, Sierra, Daniel, Greg, and Shaunda. Thanks also to Karen Pierotti for naming Upper Pangford.

A big thanks to Greg for all of the support and long conversations about plot and characters. You know this story almost as well as I do. Thank you also to my family for always cheering me on: Josie, Daniel, Will, Shannon, and Maren.

Thanks to my parents for instilling in me a love of reading and an appreciation of history. I miss you more than I can express.

And thanks to you, dear reader. You make it all worthwhile.

Discover Romance in Every Bloom

VICTORIAN VALENTINES

Don't miss out on these other romances in the Victorian Valentines series!

Violets for Veronica

Miss Sophia's Snapdragon Enigma

Lilacs for Lucy

Forget-Me-Nots for Felicity

Miss Rachel's Roses

Snowdrops for Sybil

Daphne and Her Daffodils

A Bouquet of Blue Sailors

Cecilia the Sweetbrier

www.ingramcontent.com/pod-product-compliance
Lightning Source LLC
Chambersburg PA
CBHW031044310726
48969CB00007B/2113